I0623902

Wrecked

KNIGHT PACK BOOK 1

Elissa Daye

This is a work of fiction. Names, characters, places, and incidents are products of the author's imagination or are used fictitiously and are not to be construed as real. Any resemblance to actual events, locations, organizations, or persons, living or dead, is entirely coincidental.

World Castle Publishing, LLC
Pensacola, Florida
Copyright © Elissa Daye 2019
Paperback ISBN: 9781950890088
eBook ISBN: 9781950890095
First Edition World Castle Publishing, LLC, June 10, 2019.
http://www.worldcastlepublishing.com
Licensing Notes
All rights reserved. No part of this book may be used or reproduced in any manner whatsoever without written permission, except in the case of brief quotations embodied in articles and reviews.
Cover: Melissa Davis
Editor: Maxine Bringenberg

Chapter 1

The winds howled in the pitch black that surrounded her. Brina shivered in the cold as her hair slapped angrily against her face. Even the small flashlight in her hand barely warmed her against the icy bitterness around her. She pulled her hood closer to her head and switched the light on again to shine on the path before her.

Coming here might very well have been a mistake, but she had been drawn here by some hidden force that she could not describe. The Witch's Hollow — the one place where the ghouls came out to play, or so it was said. But that wasn't what she had come here for. The spirits had brought her here, against her will. Their incessant chatter was driving her crazy.

Brina turned to the sound of a crunching footstep and shone her flashlight to find the source of the sound. Not that a little bit of light would shield her from whatever madness lay within this forest.

"Relax, Brina. It's nothing."

She continued along the path, trying to keep her thoughts from turning over all the tales of horror mixed in with the Witch's Hollow. Some of the darkest magic in the world was supposed to be within these woods. Those that practiced the dark and the light seemed to be in constant battle over these lands. Legend told that each time they fought against each other a vortex opened, bringing evil out to walk the earth. Brina wasn't entirely sure this was true, but it would explain why the woods were filled with winter ice when the lands just beyond were just starting to experience the gentle balmy fall that had followed the blazing hot summer.

Where did they want her to go? It was pretty much a straight path through the forest here, but there were a few small indentations in the grass that hinted at man-made trails that ran through. "Okay, if you're there, you'd better give me a sign." Brina stopped in her tracks and tapped her foot in slow irritation as another gust of wind shook through her. "Ugh! And hurry, before I freeze my butt off."

"Well, that would certainly be a waste," a man's voice called to her.

Brina spun around and searched her pockets for the pepper spray she was always armed with. "Who's there?" She didn't see a soul, which wasn't that odd considering voices talked to her all the time — but usually they were from beyond the grave. This one wasn't. How did she know? Because it wasn't something that popped up in her head. It was vocal, and loud enough to indicate he was not that far from her.

A man stepped out of the tree line and gave her a small nod. "This isn't a safe place for innocents."

Innocent my ass, she thought to herself. Brina was no freshman to darkness. She had been hunting it for most of her life. "I'll take my chances."

"A girl with guts; I like it."

She shone the light on his face and saw that he was grinning at her. He held his hand up to protect his eyes, but stood his ground. Brina saw a figure behind him, a shadow of sorts. "You're being watched," she warned him.

"Oh? By who?" He asked her with interest.

"Not a who, a what." She smirked at him and wondered just how much his little mind could handle, because from here she could see the creature was almost a foot behind him — the dark phantom, a chaos creature attracted to those who could easily be converted to the dark side. This man walked both sides, Brina could see that from here.

"Oh? And just what is following me?" He crossed his arms over his chest and leaned lazily against the nearest tree as he waited for her reply.

The shape floated away from him and she shook her head. "Never mind. My mistake."

Sometimes phantoms would roam aimlessly too. Perhaps the man wasn't as easily manipulated as she'd thought. Then again, it wasn't something she could figure out with a chance meeting.

"Mind if I walk with you?" he asked her quizzically.

"Why?" Brina's guard was up.

"I'm tracking something." He didn't give any other details.

"I don't run off with strangers," Brina replied, and she

started to walk away.

"I'm Killian. I live up on the hill toward the entrance."

"You're one of the Knights?" Brina asked him. At that moment she really looked him over. He looked to be about six foot tall. His eyes were indistinguishable in the dark, but if she had to guess they were hazel. His hair was short, with brown spikes that seemed to lighten slightly at the tips, as if he spent a fair amount of time in the sun. She could see just a small amount of scruff covering his face, as if perhaps he was preparing his face for the fall. Was he the kind of man who grew a beard in the winter, only to shave it off in the summer? Brina wasn't quite sure why her mind wondered these questions, as she had much more to accomplish than meeting a handsome stranger in the dark.

"Yeah, why?" He asked curiously. He was taking her in as well, which didn't surprise her. If she had to guess, Killian was a little bit of a lady's man.

"No reason." Which wasn't the truth. Not really. The spirits had told her that a Knight might join her. When she had walked from the parking lot, she had seen the family name on the sign near the house. Knight's Orchard. It didn't take a genius to figure out the correlation.

"So...?"

"So, what?" Brina asked him in irritation. He was slowing her down. She had a lot of ground to cover.

"Your name is?"

"Sabrina Moss." She was surprised to see recognition flash across his face. Not many people knew of her—only those with ties to the magical world. Brina was a psychic detective who had devoted her life to solving paranormal crime.

"What brings you to our neck of the woods, Sabrina? Demon? Vampire?" There were other creatures he could mention, but he stopped there.

"I'm not sure you want to know." She smirked and wondered who he really was.

"The woods aren't safe, Sabrina."

"Brina," she corrected him. She wasn't entirely sure why she did that. There was something about him that was familiar, even though she was sure they had never met.

"Witch's Hollow is crawling with danger tonight. You shouldn't go in."

"Damn it." Her flashlight started to flicker as an unknown source started to drain the battery.

"Not again." He apparently had experience with this occurrence.

A sudden shiver ran down her spine, as if to demonstrate Killian's words. Brina closed her eyes and summoned enough courage to get her through this. A large whoosh of air came toward them, and Brina knew it was more than just a bad sign. She moved toward Killian and reached for his arm.

When the light switched back on slightly, she saw he had a grin plastered on his face. "Don't worry, I'll keep you safe."

Brina rolled her eyes. Good grief. Ego much? "Actually, I think you might want to stand behind me."

"Oh?" His voice was curious.

The hair on the back of her neck started to stand up. She shoved the flashlight in her coat pocket and waved her hands in front of her, casting a clear net of white light that grew larger by the second. Throwing it up just in time, she deflected the burst of darkness that shot against it. The air around them started to crackle as the being that had attacked continued to pull the energy from the world around them.

"I hate energy thieves. Ugh!" Brina let her shield light the way as she looked for the creature that was sending its attacks at them.

"What the hell is that thing?" Killian pointed at the dark green creature near them.

"That thing?" Brina looked at the imp that was barely up to their knees. It was cackling wildly as it gathered enough magic for another attack. Its long ears stood up in the air in sharp points. It was a hairless creature, with big white eyes with tiny red pupils. Its teeth were long jagged spikes filled with a foul debris she could smell from here.

"Yes, what is it?"

"An imp. But not for long." Brina held one hand in front of her to steady the white shield. With the other she conjured a crackling ball of red light. The second the imp launched its next attack, Brina let it fly off the shield, then sent the red ball directly toward it. The imp yelped on impact and scampered off into the woods.

"Nasty little bastard," muttered Killian.

Brina shook her head and turned to face him. She was prepared for many things when she met his eyes. Judgment, that was the first thing she expected. Most of the world didn't believe in magic, and when they were even remotely exposed to it, they crucified the witch before she could even defend herself. Judgment was usually the beginning. Next

WRECKED

came contempt, laced with disgust. But when she looked in his eyes, she didn't see any of those things. Instead, she saw respect laced with something dark and mysterious. Was that desire?

"Yes, nasty uhm…things."

"Where do you suppose it came from?" He asked her.

"Whoever summoned me here, they probably know. But that's neither here nor there."

A loud clap sounded above them and Brina hung her head in defeat. "Seriously? Can't a girl catch a break?"

Lightning illuminated the forest briefly, alluding to the dark shapes that lingered inside the line of trees. They were being watched, but by what she couldn't quite tell. Not yet, at least. Unfortunately, it didn't look like she would find out any time soon. Large rain drops plopped down on her head — one, two, ten. Then before she knew it, the sky opened and released its fury on the ground below. She shivered, now cold and wet, standing beside a man who seemed to find every minute of this to be hilarious.

"Brrr.... Okay. I give up." She threw her hands up to the sky and turned around on the path.

"Allow me to assist you. If you parked in the lot by the orchard, I know a short cut."

Brina narrowed her eyes on him. Nothing had gone according to plan. If she followed him, she had a feeling that something else might go completely backwards, but what choice did she have? "Fine, but no funny business."

He held up his hand in front of him and made a cross over his heart. "I promise."

9

Brina walked by his side, unwilling to let him get too far ahead of her in this darkness. The only relief was the occasional burst of light that made its web across the sky. A branch whipped her in the face and she brushed it away. Where the hell had that come from? The woods were certainly high spirited, and she hadn't even made it to the Witch's Hollow yet. Perhaps another time would be better. She made a mental note to avoid the darkness next time and search in the light of day.

"So, do you always attract the paranormal?" He asked her with a slight tease to his voice.

"You know who I am. That must mean you have some experience with the paranormal yourself," she bit back.

"Oh, you could say that, but it usually stays to itself. I don't get attacked very often."

He looked at her as if he were overconfident about something, but Brina couldn't quite figure it out. She rolled her eyes to the skies above and tried to not let his cockiness get under her skin. It wasn't her fault that they didn't like to be found, nor that they seemed to be attracted to her. She always seemed to bring the wrong sort around. Such was life.

"And here we are." Killian gave her a grand flourish with his arm as they now stood right before the parking lot.

How in the world had he managed that? Seeing in the dark like that, he must have spent many a night out there exploring the woods. She found that quite curious. "Thank you."

"Any time. If you need anything else, we're right up at the house there."

"That's kind of you, but I really do need to get back on the road," she lied. The only thing she had waiting for her was an empty hotel room in Wadsworth, but he didn't need to know that.

"It was nice to meet you, *Brina*." The way he emphasized her name sent a slight shiver through her.

"You too, Killian." She watched him move toward the large house just a little further away. It was hard to tell from here, but she found herself imagining just how tight those jeans were. She felt a warm blush fill her cheeks and chided herself. "Time to go, Brina."

Chapter 2

Brina opened the door of her car and slid into the seat, ignoring the fact that she was drenched. She'd deal with the clean up later. It was time to get back to town to find a hotel. Sliding the key in place, she turned it in the ignition, but nothing happened.

"Now what the hell?"

She tried again and this time a muffled rumble started, before it faltered and sputtered. The next time she turned it, she heard a loud pop from somewhere under the hood. "That didn't sound good."

Brina put her head on the steering wheel and sighed. The goal had been to get away from here before the roads started to flood. She had seen how close they were to the water already. Her guess was the roads were often washed out. The strange thing was she had checked the weather before she'd even made her way over here. Big difference that had made, apparently. Weather was fickle like that, especially when magic was in play.

Someone or something didn't want her to go into Witch's Hollow. Was it the same thing that didn't want her car to start? It was like the universe was at odds with itself.

"If it wasn't for bad luck, I'd have no luck at all," she muttered.

Brina looked over at the large plantation style house just across the way. Several lights were on, which wasn't a huge surprise considering that it was only nine o'clock. While it was dark as pitch outside, it was still relatively early in the evening. She contemplated staying inside her car, but the more she sat there, the more the water seeped into her skin.

Maybe she could call a tow truck before it was too late. Turning on her cell phone, she waited to see if she could get a signal. One bar, two. Zero. This was definitely not her night. Brina shivered as a chill raced through her body. Sitting out here wasn't going to do her any good.

Gathering her purse, she pushed the door open and headed out into the freezing rain. By the time she made her way to large sign that read Knight's Orchard and Inn, Brina realized this didn't have to be the Greek tragedy she was making it out to be. If her luck changed, maybe they had a room available.

Brina was almost up to the steps leading into the inn when her foot got stuck in a sloshy puddle of mud. "Oh, come on!" She tried to yank her foot out, but only ended up pulling her foot out of her shoe. As she bent over to retrieve the shoe, she fell flat on her face. Brina rolled over and wiped the mud off her face. Her hands slapped the ground in frustration.

A soft chuckle erupted from behind her. "Need some help?"

"It's not funny!" Grrrr....she wanted to throw something at him, but with the ground so soft the only thing she had close to her slipped through her fingers.

"Allow me." Killian scooped her up from the ground and carried her with the greatest ease to the top of the stairs.

Brina felt something spark inside her the moment his hands touched her. When her eyes met his, she had the distinct impression that he might kiss her. Instead, he lowered her to the floor. He didn't move away as she thought he would. Instead, his eyes took in her face. He smoothed strands of wet hair from her face and smiled.

"You all right now?"

"I appear to be, but it looks like I've marked you." She bit her bottom lip. Was it just her, or did her words seem to make his eyes spark slightly?

"It'll wash." He stepped away from her now and walked back down the steps. He retrieved her shoe and handed it up to her. "Cinderella...."

Brina rolled her eyes upward. "How original."

"Would you care to come inside?" He walked around her and opened the door.

Why did she have the distinct feeling he was leading her into his lair? Maybe she should just take her chances with her car.

As if sensing her hesitation, he coaxed, "I won't bite."

Brina walked past him, and could have sworn he said, "At least not yet." She turned to find his expression had not

14

changed at all. Now her mind was playing tricks on her. She was sure of it. She stood near the door and saw the beautiful wooden floors that she was dripping water on. Brina quickly removed her other shoe. "Sorry."

"You've nothing to apologize for, Brina." His voice was gentle as took her shoe from her. "It's not like you conjured this storm."

"I didn't, but I'm not entirely convinced someone else didn't."

Killian held his hands up defensively. "Wasn't me."

"Oh, I didn't mean.... I wasn't suggesting that." She tried to find the right words, but none of them seemed to fit.

"Relax, Brina. It was a joke." His eyes held a merry glow to them.

"Right."

"So, how can I help you?"

"Well, my car won't start. I tried to get a tow truck...."

"No signal?" He crossed his arms over his chest knowingly.

"Yes...I had one earlier. It's the strangest thing." The more she thought about it, the sum of all the parts just didn't add up. Something strange was definitely happening here.

"It's just as well, really. When the rains pick up like this, there's no safe way out of here. Stay here." He left the room, and this time Brina could tell that his jeans did in fact fit him to form. What a form it was, too. As he turned around the corner, he saw her looking at him and a knowing smile slid across his face.

Brina lowered her head and started to rub her temples. What was wrong with her? She was here on a mission, not

15

for...well, whatever her mind was trying to distract her with. She needed to get a grip, real fast.

"Headache?" His voice came from the opposite side of the room.

Brina nearly jumped out of her skin. Of course, there was a hallway that separated all the rooms. He had just come in from the other side, but she hadn't heard his footsteps at all. "Goodness, you scared me there for a second."

"I'm harmless." He gave her a grin as he walked over with two large towels. "I thought you might like to dry off a bit."

"Thank you. Sorry to be such a bother."

She wrapped the largest towel around her and the scent of lavender filtered up to her noise — one of her favorite smells. Closing her eyes, she shivered slightly as she remembered the cold of the forest. While she had defended herself without a second thought, it was still an unnerving experience every single time. But it came with the territory, unfortunately.

From a long line of witches, Brina had very little choice in the path before her. Trained from an early age to track down the things that go bump in the night, she spent most of her time doing just that. The pay sucked, but that was okay. Money was never an issue. Her great grandmother had made sure her descendants would be financially set for life, so Brina had the freedom to continue the quest to fight against the things that threatened not only her way of life, but all the other light bearers that existed.

"Never a bother."

Yes, he definitely had hazel eyes. She found them incredibly revealing, as if she could see the soul that lay deep inside him. Yet there was something else inside, something he was hiding. Brina was convinced he had a secret he was keeping, but at the same point she didn't feel like it was something of grave importance to her at the moment.

"And who is this, Killian?" A female voice called from behind her.

Brina turned to see an older woman with long black hair. Even from here she could see the resemblance. This must be his....

"Mother, meet Sabrina Moss." Killian intercepted his mother. His eyes seemed to shoot her a secret message that only the two of them seemed to understand.

"I'm sorry to intrude on you. My car stalled and the roads are already washing out. Do you have a room for the night?" Brina asked her.

"I've got ten of them. Which one would you like? And I'm Amber Knight." She walked over to Brina and held her hand out to greet her.

Great. The best test of character was a handshake. Why did Brina feel like she was being sized up? She let the woman grab her hand and felt a small electric spark emit from her. Brina didn't pull away from her. Instead, she held her hand steady and gave her a polite nod. When the woman released her hand, she felt like she had failed some kind of test. "Pleased to meet you, Mrs. Knight."

"Amber," she corrected Brina. Her hazel eyes were still sizing her up. They were so much like Killian's that it was uncanny.

"Killian, have Karter help you with Ms. Moss's bags."

17

"Brina," she interjected as Killian held out his hand for her keys. Her eyes met his apologetically, but he gave her a nonchalant grin. He didn't seem to mind being her errand boy at the moment. She watched him leave the room as he went to retrieve her things.

"Yes, Brina. Do come have a hot cup of cocoa. You look half frozen." Amber led her to a small fire in one of the other rooms.

All the while, Brina was glad she had tried to dry her feet earlier. When Amber gestured for her to sit on one of the chairs before the fire, she hesitated. "Are you sure? I'd hate to get any of those wet."

"Hush now. They are just things. Now have a seat, Brina."

Brina had the feeling she was being dismissed slightly as she sat down on the small floral printed armchair. She had the distinct impression that Killian's mother did not approve of her presence. Did she know who she was too? That could be the reason right there. While Killian seemed open about the paranormal, perhaps she was closed to it. She'd have to spend more time with her to figure that out. Time wasn't something that was really on her side though. No, she'd spend one night here and then return to the next leg of her journey.

Brina stared into the flames before her. Fire was her favorite element. She loved to watch the flames dance when they were full of life. Watching them could tell you many things. When they were slow and peaceful, the air around her was calm, resolute. When they skipped all over the place, especially where there wasn't any wind to push against them, that meant something dangerous was nearby. The dark liked to manipulate the light, to bend it to its will.

"Would you care for some marshmallows?" Amber asked as she returned with a steaming mug of cocoa.

"No, plain's fine. Thank you." Brina accepted the drink and took a small sip. Hot and sweet, just the way it should be. "This is delicious."

"It's a family recipe." Amber sat down next to her. "So, what brings you to our neck of the woods? Were you trying to find Witch's Hollow?"

Well, she certainly didn't mince words. Brina sighed and held the cocoa in front of her. "I was."

"It's not safe for your kind here," Amber cautioned her. "You should probably leave as soon as you're able."

"Mother," Killian's voice came almost like a low growl.

"Excuse me. Boys." Amber stood up from the chair, watching her sons who were bringing Brina's luggage inside. "Take them to the purple room."

Boys? Neither one of the men who were now standing inside the room could be considered boys. Karter was light, where Killian was dark. His golden boy looks had probably turned many heads from the time he could form his first sentence. His eyes seemed to be blue from here, which probably sparkled in the sunlight.

Brina looked over at Killian, who seemed a little miffed at the moment. He didn't seem to like her checking his brother out at all. She had the distinct feeling that he felt he had some claim over her, which was ridiculous. Brina was a free woman. She could make her own choices. Besides, it wasn't like she planned on hooking up with either one of them. That simply wasn't in the cards for her.

She fought the sadness that usually filtered through her at the thought of sharing her life with anyone. At twenty-eight, she had nearly given up. Her work had taken her through many trials and tribulations, things that most men turned their noses up at. Even the magically inclined ones were not interested in cultivating a relationship with her. None of them could handle her dedication to her work, nor the chaos that seemed to follow her around. Two years ago, she had stopped dating altogether and thrown herself deeper into her work.

"Evening," a male voice welcomed her.

Brina turned to find a younger version of Killian greeting her. He must be in his mid-twenties, and equally attractive. How many men were there in this house? And how in the world did they all have the right to be so handsome? "Evening."

"I'm Kyle."

"Brina." She smiled and almost jumped when Killian's voice cut across the room.

"Kyle, aren't you supposed to be working?"

Kyle grinned at her. "Don't worry. He's really a pushover. Right, big brother?"

"I'm no such —"

"No need to scare the poor thing." Kyle's words seemed to hold more than humor.

What was up with these men? This house? Maybe she should try to swim her way to town. She certainly didn't want to be here if it was going to cause family drama. Brina wrapped the towel around her and stood up from the chair.

She walked over to Killian and put a hand on his arm. "Could you show me where my room is?"

He smirked slightly, but his eyes were still on his brother. When he finally looked down at her, his eyes were now gentler. "Of course, Brina. Follow me."

Brina turned to look back at his brother. "It was nice to meet you, Kyle."

"And you." He grinned at her before he left the room.

As they walked up the stairs, Brina gave in to her curiosity. "How many brothers do you have?"

"Four. They're as obnoxious as hell, too." He grinned at her.

"Must be nice."

"How's that? You've only met two of them."

"I'm an only child," Brina answered him softly.

"That sounds lonely." His voice was soft, as if he truly was thinking about how she must have felt as a child.

"At times, but I was never alone. Not really."

Killian stopped outside the second door on the right. "Your room."

"Thank you. And if I—"

"Bathroom is right across the hall. Unfortunately, you share it with the rest of the buffoons."

"And you too," Brina corrected him. Crap. Why had she said that? His eyes flashed with something she hadn't seen in quite some time. Desire. She would have to be careful with her words in the future. She didn't want to lead him on. There was nothing she could give him.

His voice was slightly gruff when he spoke again. "There

are plenty of towels in the bathroom closet. Make yourself at home, Brina."

She watched him walk away from her, and saw the stiff way he carried himself. "Killian?"

He turned around and his eyes met hers. Killian looked as if he were waiting for her to ask him inside. Her breath caught in her throat. Part of her wanted to, which caused a furious heat to fill her face. "Good night."

"Yes. I think it is. Sweet dreams, Brina."

This time she watched to see where he would walk to. When she saw him enter the last door on the right, she wondered if that was his room. Not that it meant anything. It wasn't like she was going to throw herself at him. She couldn't remember the last time she had been that impulsive. Try never. Brina sighed and turned back to her room, her mind still wandering.

Chapter 3

As Brina got herself organized for the night, she decided that maybe taking a warm shower would help remove the last of the cold dripping through her veins. It was barely October — the air shouldn't be that cold. A natural phenomenon for sure. Gathering her clothes together, she set them on the bed. She undressed quickly and laid the wet clothes out over the back of the chair, hoping they would dry before the morning. If not, she'd just ask for a plastic bag to toss them in and dry them later.

Brina slid into the bathrobe and tied the small belt around her waist. Running a brush through her hair quickly, she did a once over in the mirror. Her brown hair looked much darker when it was wet, which hid the natural red tints that had always been woven into it. Her green eyes were middle grade at best, not bright but not exactly olive colored even. Sometimes her eyes reminded her of a stormy sea, but those times were few and far between. She looked almost as she always did.

Walking to the door, she peered around it cautiously. When she didn't see another living soul — or dead, for that matter — Brina tiptoed quietly to the bathroom. Opening the door, she was surprised to see it was much larger inside than she'd thought it would be. Most bed and breakfast inns seemed to have a few smaller bathrooms which were shared among the occupants. Communal living at its best.

Brina turned the shower on and waited for it to heat up. When she saw steam rising, she stepped into the tub and pulled the shower curtain around her. The hot water was bliss compared to the icy rain outside. Showering as quickly as she could, Brina reached for the towel to dry herself. She wrapped one over her head and slid the robe over her again. Her skin was dry enough for her to get dressed in her room. Brina had not brought her clothes in here with her because she wanted to spend the least amount of time hogging the bathroom. She actually had no idea how many bathrooms there were to share. Considering that the inn was fairly empty right now, chances were they had enough for the current guests. Nevertheless, now that she was done, Brina went to make her hasty exit.

As she opened the door and stepped into the hallway, she was surprised to find Killian exiting his room. Had he heard her taking her shower and come out to check on her? Probably not, because the way he was staring at her was like a man who had not expected to find his favorite treat for dinner — surprise mingled with outright desire, something that he didn't seem capable of hiding. What she found disturbing was that her own body seemed to respond. She pulled her robe away from her slightly.

"Everything work for you?" His words seemed a little clumsy, as if he were searching for something better to say. The fact that he was staring at the small points that were almost standing at attention didn't actually make the situation any better. If anything, it made her fever rise that much more.

"Uhm...yeah. The water was hot." Oh my, why had she used that word? Now a small flush was covering her face, and she knew she couldn't turn that off any time soon. It was probably a good thing she was leaving in the morning. If she stayed, she might get in a lot of trouble.

"Good. I was just going downstairs."

They both moved at the same time, as if they were scattering in too many directions at once. Which didn't help matters, because the two of them collided into each other. Her hand pulled at the ties of her robe as she stumbled, and the front opened up, nearly exposing her naked body completely.

In an alternate dimension, Killian wouldn't have noticed the exposure, but that was definitely not this dimension. His eyes were now looking in places they should not be — not that she could blame him, for she had practically thrown herself at him. Brina tried to pull the tie closed, but she was transfixed in the spot. He was so close to her that she could almost feel his heat against her body. Her eyes met his and she saw a rawness inside them.

She forced herself to step away, even though her brain had an entirely different idea. Her fingers quickly tied her robe shut and she mumbled something barely intelligible.

"Sorry, excuse me."

His eyes shuttered as he tried to reign in something inside him. "Any time, Brina."

Brina slipped away from the hall into her room and closed the door behind her. She leaned against the door and slumped down to the ground. Laying her head on her knees, she took a deep breath. "That was a nightmare."

She groaned and shook her head. Way to go, Brina. She'd almost mauled the poor man. What was wrong with her? Every part of her seemed to throb with the pulse of her blood racing through her heart. Something inside her felt like it was waking up, something that had been long dormant. She couldn't quite describe the feeling, but the moment she had found herself nearly in his arms, every inch of her started to throb with the rush of blood coursing through her veins. Brina did not understand the magnetic pull she was feeling.

"Get a grip," she chided herself.

Brina jumped as a knock sounded on her door. She stood up and opened the door to find Killian standing outside. The words were caught in her throat when she saw the raw desire in his eyes. "Yes?"

"I just wanted to say...."

Brina waited with bated breath to hear what he could possibly have to say to her at this moment in time. His hand reached for hers and brought it to his mouth. His lips tickled her skin with their velvety smoothness, and a jolt of electricity shot through her body.

"Good night, Brina," his mouth whispered against her hand.

Her skin tingled and something took over her. When he released her hand, Brina stepped closer to him, so that she was just a few inches away. She raised her head up and gazed into his eyes that now almost looked golden the closer she moved toward him. Her hands reached up to pull his face down to hers and she kissed him.

Brina felt him stiffen against her before he pulled her closer to him. His lips were warm against hers, with a silky smoothness that made her want to melt like a stick of butter in his arms. A web of desire threaded its way inside her when he deepened the kiss. Oh, how easy it would be to fall into his arms, but reality started to trickle back into her mind. She was about to push away from him when a cough sounded in the hallway behind them.

"Oh, excuse me. Didn't see you there." Kyle's face held a half-contained grin.

"Kyle," Killian's voice bit out angrily.

"Yes, brother?" Kyle's voice was filled with mischief.

"Did you need something?"

"I was just heading to bed."

"Then get there," his voice gritted out. When Kyle didn't move, Killian glared at him. "Anything else?"

"Mother asked me to retrieve you." Kyle relayed the summons before heading off down the hallway to climb the stairs to the third floor.

"Damn it."

Killian's hands released her and Brina was suddenly filled with a sense of loss. She could not explain the feelings that were coursing through her right now. Making sure she

27

was completely covered, she started to retreat inside herself the minute his hands left her. Shame filled her for throwing herself at a complete stranger. She was about to step into her room when she heard Killian's voice.

"Oh, hell." He moved her into her room and closed the door behind them.

"What are you doing, Killian?" Brina's voice was filled with shock when his body seemed to stalk hers. Her eyes met his and she saw a light flash inside them. Her breath caught in her throat when she found the solid door behind her back.

"Giving us some privacy." His hand rose up to her face and his thumb gently stroked her cheek.

"For what?" She almost squeaked.

"This."

His lips brushed against hers gently and he coaxed her mouth open. When his tongue slid inside her mouth, Brina sighed against him. She wrapped her arms around his neck and pulled him closer to her. His hands were at her sides, firmly planted against the door behind her. The kiss seemed to last forever, but in reality, it was merely seconds before he let her go. When he moved away from her, she already mourned the loss of his warmth.

"Good night, Brina."

She looked down at the floor through half-closed eyes as disappointment and a little bit of shame floated across her thoughts. What was wrong with her? Brina wasn't the kind of woman to throw herself at a man, and here he was essentially pushing her away when he could easily have his way with her.

His thumb stroked her cheek again. "Look at me, Brina."

Brina's eyes slowly traveled up his body until they came into contact with his own eyes. "Yes, Killian?"

"I would love to finish this, Brina. But not until you're sure."

He stepped away from her and moved to open the door. She moved out of his way so that he could make his retreat. The door closed quietly behind him.

Was he saying he wanted her? Her heart skipped in her chest and she sucked in her breath. He was right. They had known each less than a few hours. This wasn't something she should just jump into. She was here on a mission, not for a hookup. The little voice in her head whispered, *Why not both?*

"Get a grip, Brina. You can't just jump the poor man."

Was that a chuckle she heard? Could things get any more embarrassing? What was she going to do? Brina walked over to the bed and sat down on the edge. Things were certainly not going according to plan.

Brina had come here when she had been visited by a spirit that was adamant that she come help the light workers near Witch's Hollow. The spirit told her that the witches were being hunted one right after the other, and while the attacks seemed to come from some kind of dark magic, it was less than likely that the witches who worked on the other side of the line were behind it. This was something else entirely. She had been sent here to figure that out — that should be the priority. The only problem was, the minute she met Killian something in her head seemed out of focus. Or perhaps it was the other way around, actually. For some reason, she was drawn to him

29

in a way that simply didn't hold up to any rationale. Perhaps some things could not be explained.

Brina sighed. It was time to push him out of her thoughts for now. She walked over to the dresser and quickly put on her sleepwear. The silky tank and shorts were just the right amount for her right now, because her body seemed to be filled with a heat that resonated from her toes all the way up the hair that was still drying from her shower. Brina made her way to the bed and slid beneath the covers, hoping to get some sleep so that she could make her way out of here in the morning. Avoiding temptation would probably be for the best.

Chapter 4

As Brina fell asleep, her dreams were plagued with the handsome man who had kissed her until her senses had fled her body. His hands were all over her, stoking the fires that had been dormant for so long. The images flashed through her head at such a rate that her mind could not keep up with them. When she awoke unexpectedly, Brina found her entire body was throbbing in anticipation. Desire coiled through her body painfully, and Brina knew there was only one cure for it.

Squeezing her eyes shut, she tried to force herself to go back to sleep. Her attempt failed miserably. Was he having trouble sleeping too? Did his body seem drawn to hers the way she was to him?

Brina pushed away from her bed and started to pace the room. If—a big if—if she went to his room, what would happen? Would she just throw herself in his arms and forget the consequences? Would he turn her away? Shouldn't he? Honestly, for all he knew, she could be some crazy woman who would murder him in his sleep. The same could be said for him, she supposed. There was great risk involved for both of them. The more she paced, the more she had almost talked herself out of doing something she couldn't undo. But then she remembered the way she had felt the instant his mouth had touched her hand. That kind of spark was rare. Fated even, some might say. Brina had never felt that before.

Another few laps back and forth and Brina was still weighing her options. Her brain was trying to rationalize everything. Her heart won out as it bullied her conscience to the back of her mind.

Brina stepped into the hallway, and took a small breath as she slowly made her way down to the door she had seen him enter earlier. As she stood outside she stared at it, wondering what exactly she should do next. Knock? She gulped slightly. What if everyone else heard it?

She stood there with her fist poised at the door, ready to make its move, but she couldn't seem to do it. Closing her eyes, she let out a slow breath and told herself this was exactly why she never made it very far with other men. She was afraid of the risk.

A soft click interrupted her thoughts, and her eyes flew open when she heard a door sliding open. She was about to turn tail and run when her eyes met Killian's.

"Brina?" His voice was soft and almost wary.

"I...." She fought the urge to gulp. Killian was only wearing a pair of red boxers. The body that had worn his clothing so well earlier was even more inspiring to look upon without the material hiding him. "Couldn't sleep."

He smiled knowingly at her. "Neither could I."

Standing outside his door, she wasn't sure whether she should ask if she could come in, invite him to her room, or just sputter something about maybe asking for some random thing that might help her sleep, like warm milk or a snack of some kind.

Thankfully, he took the lead. His hand reached out to hers and he led her into his room beside him. He closed the door behind them, and she heard the sound of a lock clicking into place. When he saw her surprise, he grinned at her. "I have four brothers. They tend to think they can bother me at all hours of the night."

"Oh." So, what did that mean? Brina was trying to figure out what came next. Her timid nature rose to the surface once more, and she felt like she had lost all power of verbal communication. She looked away from him and tried to conjure the bravery that had sent her to his door in the first place.

"Brina...." His voice was close to her, and it sounded like he was demanding something.

Her eyes snapped up and found the delicate flame that seemed to burn in his own. "Yes, Killian?"

"Why are you here?" He asked her.

"Here?" Here as in Witch's Hollow, or here as in...well, his bedroom.

He moved closer to her, like a predator stalking its prey. Heat filled her face as she thought how delicious it would be to be devoured by him. She imagined his lovemaking was masterful. Clearly, he wasn't talking about her trip to find the culprit responsible for...what was that thing responsible for now? Rational thoughts seem to evaporate from her mind when his eyes flashed like amber before her. She moistened her lips with her tongue and closed her eyes to try to focus.

"You have to tell me, Brina." Killian's mouth was now at her ear as he walked behind her. She felt his hands slide around her stomach and she melted against him. His breath was hot on her neck and she gasped slightly. His hands roamed up her belly as he massaged her skin gently.

"I couldn't stop...." Daydreaming? Thinking about him? Wanting to taste him?

"What do you want, Brina?" His whisper against her ear had the same effect as the gentle kiss that fluttered against her neck.

"*You*," she whispered. She felt him stiffen behind her, as if her words had shaken him to the core. His hands gripped her stomach and pulled her tight against him.

"There are things you should know, Brina." He pulled back a little, and she missed his heat against her.

Brina turned around to face him. "Are you married?"

"Married?" He chuckled. "No."

"Have a girlfriend?"

"No...."

"A boyfriend?" Yes, that had happened to her before.

"What?" He held up his hands and waved that away quickly.

"So, what's the problem?" Brina felt like some stranger had taken over her body. Was she literally trying to talk him into sleeping with her? Oh, Goddess help her.

"I'm not like other men, Brina."

Her eyebrow rose curiously. "Oh?"

"I'm actually surprised you didn't already know." His hand reached out for hers and he kissed it before placing it on his chest.

The moment her fingers were over his heart, she closed her eyes. Flashing images echoed in her head. Hints of fur, a glint of teeth. Brina saw a creature sliding through the shadows, seen and unseen by the world around it. She opened her eyes and looked up at him. "You're a werewolf?"

"Yes." His jaw seemed hardened now, as if he were braced for her rejection.

"So?" She smirked at him. There were far worse things he could be.

"I'm not like other men, Brina. I can't just sleep with whomever I want, not when it's my time."

Time? What was he talking about? She glanced at him curiously. "Time?"

"When we are younger, we can be as careless as we like, Brina. When our beasts reach a certain age, we're no longer able to run wild. We must choose a mate to live out the rest of our lives with."

"Oh...." So, he was saying that they couldn't sleep together. Brina felt like cold water had been thrown at her face. He didn't really want her. "I understand."

"Do you?" His body moved effortlessly across the floor and he swept her against him again. "Make no mistake, Brina. I want you more than the air I breathe. Every inch of me wants to mark you as my own."

35

Her breath caught in her throat. It wasn't fear that pulsed through her, but a raw desire to find out just how he intended to make his mark. Her eyes met his again, and she was transfixed in the moment where destiny seemed to be calling her home. Her grandmother had always told her she would know the *one*. The old woman had foreseen it long ago, telling her that when she did she could not let that moment pass her by. Brina had never understood it until now.

"Will you?" she whispered.

He blinked in confusion. "Will I what, Brina?"

"Make me yours." She nibbled on her bottom lip and waited to see what he had to say about that.

"I'm not sure you really understand...." He ran a hand through his hair, as if he were trying to maintain some semblance of control.

"I do. I think I've been waiting for you." She stepped closer to him and put her hands on his chest. His muscles bunched up in reflex.

"Brina...." His voice was almost a soft growl. "Don't touch me right now."

"Why not, Killian?" She whispered as her fingers slid down his stomach.

"I'm trying to do the right thing," he cautioned her.

Brina withdrew her hands and her eyelids shuttered. Had she been wrong? "I see."

She felt tears building behind her eyes, and she felt even more foolish. Turning away from him, she started to walk to the door. Brina's hand had just touched the knob when his voice stopped her.

"Brina."

"Do you know how hard it was for me to walk down this hallway, Killian?" she whispered. "I've never wanted anyone the way I want you. It defies reason." She turned around to face him, determined to let him know just how he made her feel. "Do you know how hard it is to find someone who accepts you? I do. I come from a long line of witches who refuse to back down from anything. You probably couldn't handle that."

"I could," he argued.

"I'm incredibly complicated to deal with. Mornings are a pain in the ass until I have my coffee. I get up at all hours of the night to deal with the dead. I hunt for the truth whether that fits in with a man's schedule or not. I'm a nightmare."

"I see." His eyes seemed to have a merry light to them.

"I'm a *real* mess. But I'm your mess, if you want it." She moved closer to him, turning the tables on him without even thinking about it. "Or are you not man enough to handle it?"

Desire flashed in his eyes. "Brina, I don't think—"

"I see...your loss."

She turned away from him and made a hasty retreat from his room. She knew the terms. He had literally spelled them out for her. If she slept with him, there would be no turning back. Clearly, she was not sure what he wanted. Could she blame him though? They barely knew each other.

When she slid into her room, she locked the door behind her. She couldn't handle one more inch of rejection. Brina walked over to her bed and curled up in a ball as the tears fell down her face. Clearly the madness of the moment had taken over. The best thing she could do was to get out of here as soon as possible. The more distance she put between them, the easier it would get. Brina knew that she would never feel this magnetic pull with anyone else. It didn't take a fortune teller to convince her. When she finally tired of crying, she slipped into a tormented sleep.

Chapter 5

The next morning, Brina quickly packed her things. As quietly as she could, she moved her bags down to the first floor. She was thankful that Killian was nowhere around. If she were lucky, today the car would start. She was half tempted to cast a fortune spell to make it so, just so she could avoid making a bigger fool of herself.

"Leaving so soon?" a voice called across the foyer as she was rolling her bags.

Brina nearly jumped out of her skin. She had not seen Karter sitting on the chair near the fireplace. "I'd like to get a head start if my car actually starts."

"Pity." He smirked slightly. "You know, he's not always such a brute."

Brina blushed. "It has nothing to do with Killian."

"Right. Nothing at all." His voice was teasing her slightly, but his eyes were serious. "I can take a look at your car if you like."

"If it wouldn't be too much trouble." Brina gave him a weak smile.

"Not at all. Always happy to help a damsel in distress." He rose from the chair and walked over to where she stood. He offered his arm to her. "My lady."

A growl sounded from the stairs above them. "Karter... what are you doing?"

Brina wanted to sink into the ground and disappear. She didn't want to see him, be anywhere near him, or breathe the air he breathed. Ignoring the battle that was about to ensue between the siblings, Brina walked away and continued to take her bags out to the car. She made it out to the porch before she heard a loud exchange behind her.

Closing her eyes, she tried not to care about whatever they were discussing. He had made it clear last night that he wasn't looking for a mate. He wanted her, but not forever. At least that's what she walked away with. "Men."

As she made her way across the stones, at least there was enough light to keep her from sinking into the mud like last night when she had missed the path completely. When she got to the gravel, she started to roll her bags again. At this point she didn't care how messy her bags were. She just wanted to get the hell out of there so she could check this off as the worst experience of her life. Tossing her bags into the trunk, she almost ripped her nail as one of the handles slammed against her hand. "Damn it."

"Need some help?"

Freaking a.... How many men were here? She turned to find another brother staring at her with a mischievous smile plastered on his face. "And you are?"

"Kameron." He appeared to be a little older than Killian. His hair was a dark brown with reddish hue. His eyes were bright green, which suited the friendly smile on his face. While Killian was well-built, his brother was a giant. His arms were the size of a thigh, and well maintained, as she could see the way the T-shirt fell against his muscles. Handsome was apparently in their DNA.

"I see. That leaves one other, I think." Brina sighed. "Can you help me get my car started?"

"I can, but you won't get very far."

"Why's that? Do you think he will stop me?" Brina's chin jutted out defiantly.

"No, but the roads might. It rained most of the night." His eyes twinkled merrily.

She cursed under her breath. "Of course."

"He's not all that bad, you know."

"What is it with all of you?" Brina stomped her foot on the ground and a small drop of mud splashed up on her hand. Angry tears formed in her eyes, as the emotions that she had been trying to keep well contained were swimming to the top.

Kameron looked at her with concern. "Did he hurt you?"

"No," she denied.

"I'll kill him. Fucking brute." Kameron ground one of his fists into his hand. The satisfied look on his face only led her to believe he liked to fight with his brothers.

"No... he didn't hurt me."

"Then why are you crying?" He asked her seriously.

"Gah! Men!" After throwing her purse in the trunk and

stuffing her keys into her jacket pocket, Brina slammed the door shut on her car. She held up her hand as she started to walk away from him. "Just leave me alone."

Brina almost stomped away from him. She didn't want to deal with any of them at the moment. It was bad enough that the road was flooded. Brina decided to do the one thing she had come here to do. She walked down the path that would lead her toward Witch's Hollow. At least she could do what it was she actually came here to do—if she could forget the hazel eyes that seemed to be stained into her memory.

She felt the air change around her slightly the further she walked. Brina made it to the path where she had run into Killian the night before. At the time, she hadn't even thought to be afraid of him. Perhaps she should have run as fast as her feet could carry her, but even then, she had been starting to feel the magnetic pull between them.

She shivered slightly as the cold returned, which turned her thoughts away from the handsome werewolf who had been so close to changing the course of her fate. If their fates weren't destined to cross.

"What is going on here?"

Brina felt an energy source pulsing around her. It seemed to be drawing her in deeper into the forest. Was that where Killian had come from last night? Was it possible that he knew what was going on in these woods? Not that she would be asking him about that any time soon.

Brina left the safety of the path and stepped into the cover of the trees. As she walked, Brina found little shapes carved into wood and stone throughout the dense forest.

The triquetra, a three-cornered knot that had no beginning or end, was a protective symbol used by the lightworkers here. It stood for protection, and was one of the strongest symbols of the Triple Goddess. While this was supposed to keep the woods safe from the outside world, it was also being countered by something very dark and evil. Brina could not quite put her finger on it. That darkness could be the exact thing that had sent the imp to attack her last night.

Even though she had been walking for an hour or more, Brina was still not finding anything substantial. Brina pulled her phone out of her pocket and took a quick photo of some of the symbols. She got a little closer and found a small pouch on the ground by a tree nearby. Picking up a stick, she poked at it and found blood seeping through the cloth. She sighed and shook her head. "When will they learn?"

Using the same stick to dig a small hole, Brina started to bless the dirt below. She opened the bag and saw some kind of rodent, or the remnants of one, that had been sacrificed probably the night before. Brina could feel the dark energy siphoning from it and held her hands over it. She cleansed the contents with a healing white light and said a silent prayer for the animal that had lost its life so brutally. When she was done, the dark feeling had lessened. Reaching inside her other pocket, she retrieved the small packet of Celtic sea salt that she always carried with her. She tossed a few granules over the bag and continued to pray over it. When she was done, Brina filled the hole around it and buried the poor creature.

She reached into her shirt and pulled her pentacle up to her lips to kiss it. Then she let it fall closer to her as she looked up to the sky above her. "As above, so below. As below, so above. So, mote it be."

Brina felt the fingers of light touch her neck and knew she was no longer alone. "Hello?"

The voice that had led her here was floating closer to her ear. *Danger lurks.*

The ghostly whisper was for her ears alone. The voice was female, almost old and brittle. While some were attached to corporeal forms, not all of them were. Brina much preferred the voice to the projection, although sometimes it was tricky to ascertain if the entity speaking to her was from the light or dark, when all she had was a voice to go on. It took a lot of gut instinct to figure it out.

Darkness.

"I can see that. What do you want me to do?"

Find the one.

"Which one?" She really hated when the spirits spoke in riddles. Sometimes they could see the natural world better than the humans could, but they refused to give more than what was needed.

"Hello?"

The cold fingers no longer tickled her skin. Instead, the world went back to the way it had been moments before. Clearly, she wasn't going to get anymore from the ghost at the moment. What she had found out was that whatever was making the woods so dangerous to the lightworkers was one person. Unfortunately, she had to agree with the spirit. The longer she stayed within the forest, the easier it was to see that it was filled with something dangerous. She almost felt as if she were marked with the evil eye right now. Every step she took seemed to be punctuated with a foggy feeling. The forest was starting to affect her. Today was not the day to tackle this. She had no choice but to return to the inn.

As if to indicate her body's willingness to return, her stomach started to rumble, reminding her that she hadn't eaten a thing. She didn't really want to head back. Pulling out her phone, she looked up the road conditions in the area. The text alerts on the page indicated that the road would probably be safe to travel tomorrow.

"Ugh. Now, I just have to make it through one more day."

Brina put her phone back in her pocket, amused by the fact that last night her phone had not worked, yet today it had four bars. The cloud cover last night must have affected it. She crossed her fingers that the weather stayed constant and steady until she could find a place in town. While she would still need to investigate Witch's Hollow, she was pretty sure she could use the entrance on the other side of the town.

Chapter 6

At the house Killian was doing his best not to tear his brother to shreds. "What the hell do you think you're doing, Karter?" He ran his hands through his hair as anger shook him to the core.

"Well, if you don't want her, she's fair game, right?" His voice was teasing him, but Killian didn't seem to catch the humor.

"No, she's not!" Killian's fingers bit into the palms of his hand. He was having a serious control issue right now. Usually he was pretty even keeled, but the minute Brina had touched him something inside him had snapped. His control had unraveled and he wanted to make his claim over her. But he couldn't let the beast inside take over all his senses. Killian was raised better than that.

"He sure is testy," grumbled Kyle.

"It's his own damn fault. Had the perfect opportunity and tossed it out like trash." Kam had just come into the door, slamming it behind him. "You know you're an ass, right?"

"I didn't throw her out." Killian narrowed his eyes on Kameron, his oldest brother and biggest pain in his ass.

"You might as well have. Poor thing was a little peeved to learn that she wouldn't be able to drive away today." Kam shook his head. "Funny thing, the weather. Did Mother have anything to do with that?"

"No. Quite the opposite." His mother came into the living room. "I tried to talk some sense into him. Apparently, he listened."

"You're no fun!" Kyle plopped down on the couch and crossed his arms. "You do know the leader goes first, right? What about the rest of us? We're all waiting too."

Killian sniffed in slight irritation. "It's not my fault you peaked early."

Kyle held his hands up, "Well, some of us are downright —"

"Sex-crazed?" suggested Killian, then he saw his mother shake her head at him. "Sorry, Mother."

"You should be. You have to choose wisely, boys. Not just any woman will do. This is the one you'll be with for the rest of your mortal lives." Amber Knight walked across the room almost regally. She sat down in one of the small armchairs and looked over the bunch of disgruntled men in the room. "Waiting never hurt anyone."

"Woman, what are you teaching those boys?" Kenton Knight walked into the room. He kissed his wife on the top of her head and turned to see a room filled with men in various degrees of annoyance. Then he turned back to their mother. "What did you do, Amber?"

"Don't blame me if he has a conscience," she chided her husband.

Killian refused to meet his mother's eyes. He had a conscience, but he also had a growing need inside him that did not want to be ignored. Killian wasn't sure how much longer he could continue to hold out. Especially considering the lack of interest in the rest of the female population.

"And what's wrong with this young lady...there is a young lady, I presume."

"She's a witch—a nosy one at that." Amber crossed her arms over her chest.

Kenton almost lost it completely. His laughter boomed around the room. "Woman...so are you! That didn't stop me."

Amber narrowed her eyes on him. "Are you calling me nosy?"

Kenton was the only one of the Knight men who wasn't afraid of Amber Knight. He gave it right back to her. "Yes. Nosy, opinionated, and sometimes manipulative."

Killian and the rest of his brothers averted their gazes, all of them knowing that all hell was about to break loose. In a matter of one, two, three—

"KENTON KNIGHT! Bite your tongue! I won't have some three-ring circus erupt in my household. Do you know that woman has a reputation?" She glared at him.

"Oh?" Karter's eyebrow rose curiously. "That could be interesting. Maybe I should throw my hat into the ring."

"Shut it!" Killian growled at him. There was no way in hell he would let any of his brother's lay claim to Brina. They could go find their own. If he couldn't have her, none of them

48

would.

"Well, if she turned you down, I might still have a chance." Karter was clearly having fun stirring the nest. Several voices were now talking at once, all of them trying to get control over the conversation.

"She didn't turn me down."

The room went quiet, so quiet a feather could have dropped and everyone would have heard it. Six collective pairs of eyes were now trained on him in slight fascination. Killian let out a loud huff of air and clenched his teeth. His brothers were counting on him to choose a mate soon. His mother was counting on him not to make the wrong choice. His father was the only one who seemed to care about what he wanted.

"And you turned her away, Killian?" Kenton's voice was soft as he tried to determine his son's state of mind.

"Yes."

"Uhm, I've got some work to do in the...back room." Karter was the first one to slip out of the room.

"Oh, right. Me too." Kyle slid off the couch and quickly followed after him.

Killian looked over at Kam, waiting to see if he was going to go too. "Kam?"

"What? I'm fine where I am."

"Kameron Knight," Amber chided him.

"Right. But before I go, perhaps you should know your castoff is heading into Witch's Hollow." He left the room muttering about his jackass brother. "Has a perfectly willing woman and doesn't know what to do with her."

Killian was about to go after him when his father put a hand on his arm. "Let me go."

"Sit, Killian," he ordered him.

Killian did as his father asked him. He moved to the couch and almost threw his body onto it. He leaned forward and slumped over his knees. What was he supposed to do? Kam was right. He had literally tossed her out like the trash. Killian had sensed her anguish through the walls.

"What do you need to do, Killian?" Kenton asked him.

"What do you mean?" Killian looked up at his father.

"What does your beast tell you?"

"Kenton," Amber interrupted him. "You can't suggest he go after her."

"Woman, I've been lenient on many things. Let you run this house as you saw fit, supported your every decision. But this I cannot abide. If I had listened to my family, you and I would never have happened. This family would not exist. Even if it meant losing my pack, I would do it a hundred times over."

Tears filled Amber's eyes. "I didn't mean to...."

"Do you trust him?" Kenton asked her.

"Well, yes. But it's not him that I don't trust." Amber tried to wave away her husband's words.

"Do you love me, wife?" Kenton knelt down in front of her.

"Yes. More than anything." She smiled at him and closed her eyes. It was as if she had realized finally what her husband was trying to say. "Killian, you do not need my approval. You never have. If she is the one you want, above all else, then you have my blessing."

Killian let out a deep breath. He was so conflicted he couldn't sort out what his human heart wanted versus what the beast beneath needed. More than likely, he had ruined his chances anyway. He had not handled the situation very well at all.

"It's probably just as well that she's leaving." Killian rose from the couch and moved to the other side of the room.

Amber rose and put her hand on his arm. "I've been selfish."

Killian put his hand over hers. "No. You just care about us."

"You're my children. You'll always be my baby." Amber pinched his arm. "Don't you dare roll your eyes at me, Killian."

"I'm thirty-three, hardly a baby." He smirked at her.

"And not in your prowling days any more. As much as I dread the day you leave our house, all of you, it's time for you to find the next stage of your life."

"I wouldn't wait too much longer, Killian. Your brothers might skin your hide," his father cautioned him.

"Well, if one of them had won the rites of passage, then they would have been able to go first. It's not my fault," he grumbled.

His brothers were always giving him grief. Amazingly enough, Kam, who was thirty-five, was less interested in finding his mate than his youngest brother, who was twenty-five. Of course, Kam had been able to prowl longer than the others. Unfortunately, there was no rhyme or reason where their beasts were concerned. When they were ready for their mates, there didn't seem to be any reasoning with them. Even now he felt the wild growing stronger within him, if that were even possible. His wolf spirit wanted its mate, and would not be satisfied until he had her.

"Nevertheless, your lack of a mate does put a damper on them. As much as your mother wants to keep you all near, there is a reason we had the separate houses built," Kenton reminded him.

"And what if my journey takes me farther?" Killian asked them.

"Then we will have to keep in touch." Amber wrapped her arms around him and hugged her son.

Killian turned around and wrapped his arms around her. "You're really okay with this?"

"Yes. But she'd better be good to you, or I'll hex her," Amber threatened.

"Women...." Kenton rolled his eyes as he shook his head.

"I'll have you know it's actually women who run this world," Amber chided him as she walked over to kiss him on the cheek.

Kenton refused to rise to the challenge. Instead he chuckled softly. "Yes, dear."

"What are you waiting for, Killian?" Amber asked him.

"She's probably upset with me."

Kam had just re-entered the room. "You think?"

"Kam, so help me!" Killian was half tempted to lay his toothy grinned brother out flat, but at that moment the hairs on the back of his neck rose. Trouble. His eyes met Kam's and found the same thing reflected there.

"I'll get the others. Go, Killian. She needs you."

Killian didn't wait any longer. He ran out the door and raced to the woods, where he could transform without anyone seeing him.

Chapter 7

Brina looked around her. Was she lost? She was pretty sure this was the way she had come in — wasn't it? The more she looked around her, the more she realized that nothing looked familiar at all. How was that possible?

Trees lined the area to her right. None of them had the symbols of protection. While the sun was shining, the cold air bit against her lungs. A fog seemed to cover the ground, which was not uncommon for fall, but this felt heavy and mysterious. Was this part of the magic of the area?

She reached her hand down to feel the energy at her feet. The fog didn't feel negative, nor did it feel positive. The energy was somewhere in the middle, which in itself wasn't anything to worry about. The absence of life, however, that did make her slightly cautious. But it wasn't enough to make her turn around, so she continued to walk through it.

As Brina continued to walk through the tree line, her thoughts turned to Killian. She had never met a man who made her blood boil just from proximity. Not one to jump into things, she was actually surprised that she had practically thrown herself at him. Okay, so not practically, but actually. Brina had actually thrown herself at him, and he had turned her down. That kind of made her feel justified in keeping to herself even more. Her feelings were more than troubled — they were mixed up, torn, battered, and bruised. She should have expected that, though.

Putting herself out there wasn't something that came easily to her. Experience had taught her that the only person she could ever trust was herself, although after last night, she was starting to doubt that as well. Brina sighed. This was a whole tangled mess; one she would hopefully be able to push far from her mind when she left this place. If not, she could always drink herself into oblivion.

"But you don't drink," she reminded herself. Right. Well, maybe she should start. Maybe that would make the madness of the moment settle to a low annoyance, a blip on the radar of massive mistakes she'd made in her lifetime. She had a fair share of those. Mostly because she went on fool's errands, chasing one paranormal creature after another, solving crimes committed against them that normal law forces wouldn't even touch.

Call it paranoia or disbelief, but the law never seemed too interested in helping when anything paranormal was involved. If it was something that fell out of the normal mold of the world around them, they had trouble understanding it. It was far easier for her to understand. She lived it, every day of her life. When spirits called, she answered. When witches were being hunted, she was there to bring them justice, no matter what it took. Someone had to.

As far as the other creatures that went bump in the night, Brina found it was not usually them that created the problems. It was normally regular mortals that got off on killing innocent people. These so-called normal people had trouble accepting anything that scribbled outside their lines. Acceptance wasn't something that was embroidered into their moral codes. Which was unfortunate, because there was so much more beauty in the world than their eyes could see.

"Where am I?" She put her hands on her hips and took a deep breath. The more her thoughts raced, the harder it was to keep track of where she was. Brina knew it all went right back to Killian and his sexy eyes that had called out to her like a beacon in the night. She felt like she could see the universe reflected inside them. Was that even possible?

Come.

Brina turned to the sound of a male voice. She couldn't make out from where it resonated. It wasn't one she had heard before, either. Part of her knew better than to chase after it, but the rest of her was too curious to fight the feeling.

This way.

The voice came from the left, a few feet up. Brina squinted her eyes and thought she saw a large shape of a man. She knew he wasn't with the living, but that didn't worry her any. Spirits were something she dealt with all the time. At the moment, her inner radar wasn't alerting her to any danger, so she walked closer to the spirit.

The closer she got to it, the more it seemed to pull her

further across a clearing. It stood by the gate to a fence. As she moved closer to the gate, her mind started to get a fuzzy feeling. Warning bells started to go off in her head, but an overwhelming need to follow the spirit took over.

The man was like a pied piper. He played his flute so well that innocent people were corrupted by its song. Brina put her hand on the gate and started to open it. A sharp pain erupted in her side, as if she were being punished for not moving faster.

Hurry, the spirit commanded her. Her mind seemed to not be her own. Like a puppet being moved by invisible strings, she continued to move forward.

Brina stepped through the gate and the world seemed to slip away from her. Her hands and feet moved on their own volition. Across the field she seemed to float, to where the sounds of roaring water barely broke into her conscience. She could only see in front of her, like a hollowed tunnel vision that blocked out all the sights and sounds around her. Only one objective mattered — reaching the water. For what? That didn't seem to matter. All she had to do was get there. One foot in front of the other, her mission engraved into every inch of her consciousness.

Her feet moved across the muddy banks, sloshing in the mud as she put the first foot into the water. She felt a small smile slide across her face as she waded deeper into the water.

Nearly there. The voice sounded almost gleeful. It celebrated something she did not understand. At that moment, all she could do was continue her task. She moved slowly in the water, almost stumbling in the slow rapids that were flowing down around her calves.

From the water she saw a shape on the other side of the banks. A grey wolf stood on its haunches. It howled and a few other howls answered it from somewhere in the distance. Brina blinked, but the spell that was woven over her was far too powerful for her to break. She didn't even hear the splash of water behind her.

When two strong arms wrapped around her, Brina struggled against them. The drive to keep moving into the water was so deeply ingrained in her that her body was fighting to move forward. Water splashed around them as her body fought for every inch of control.

"Damn it, Brina." Killian hoisted her out of the water and threw her over his back as he carried her from the water.

Fight. The spirit was angry. Its mission had been disrupted.

Brina struggled against Killian, not recognizing anything but the voice that was egging her on. Her hands pummeled his back, while her legs kicked behind her. She nearly unbalanced Killian in her efforts, but his arms held her tight.

When Killian finally managed to get to the bank, he lowered her to the ground. Three wolves raced closer, but Killian waved them off. "I've got it from here."

The wolves grunted and growled slightly, as if they disagreed. Killian's voice was close to anger this time.

"I don't need your help. No, I'm not going to screw it up. And shut up, Karter."

The lightest wolf bared its fangs at him slightly, and its tongue dipped out of its mouth.

"You know I could still skin you."

A slight snort erupted from the wolf before he raced after the other two. Killian shook his head at them before looking down at the woman in his lap. He stroked her face and tried to get her to come back from the dark reverie she was trapped inside.

Brina was still lost inside herself. She barely recognized the voice calling out to her. When Killian put his hands on her face, she fought against it. The zombie state had taken her in far too fast. She felt like she was trapped inside herself.

"Brina, you have to fight it. Come back to me," he tried to coax her. None of his words seem to have any effect on her, so Killian did the only thing left.

When Killian's lips touched hers, Brina felt a part of herself warm. A small heat grew inside her, and she was finally able to blink her eyes. The longer he kissed her, more of her came alive. Her lips started to move on their own volition, no longer controlled by the haunting magic of the glen, but the power of the desire that was building slowly inside her. The hands that were trapped against his chest started to pull his wet shirt into her hands. When his tongue slipped inside her mouth, Brina closed her eyes and relaxed against his lap.

Killian removed his mouth and whispered. *"Brina?"*

Her eyes flew open; her faculties had finally returned. What the hell had happened? And what was she doing here in his arms, wet for the second time in two days? Memories from the night before came crashing to the forefront and she started to push against his chest. "Let me go."

As if startled by the turnaround of events, Killian cursed softly. He released her reluctantly. "Brina...."

Brina pushed up from his lap and brushed some of the mud from her jeans. "Damn it."

Brina kicked at the water near the bank, looking for some kind of object to toss at his head. Instead, she settled for walking up the bank. She didn't even turn to look back at him. This was his fault. If she hadn't been so distracted by him, her senses would have worked better. Brina was smarter than this. She knew she shouldn't have followed the voice — it defied every inch of her training. But all of that seemed to fly out the door, just because her emotions were all over the place. She wished she had never followed the lead to Witch's Hollow. It had been nothing but trouble.

As she trudged through the grass, she realized she had absolutely no idea where she was. She put her hand in her pocket and retrieved her phone to at least try to get a coordinate. The phone was dripping wet and refused to power on. "What the hell!"

"Brina."

She jumped when his voice came from right behind her. Stealthy, she'd give him that. Perhaps that was the werewolf in him. "Go away, Killian. You've already made your point clear."

Killian growled and yanked her back to him. "I don't think I have."

Brina put a hand on his shoulder and tried to push him away, but Killian threw her over his shoulder again. This time he held her so tightly Brina gave up the fight and wondered what in the world he was doing. "Put me down."

He never answered, just kept carrying her across the

clearing, to where she did not know. She finally gave up and just relaxed against him, wondering where he had gotten all his strength from. She wasn't a large woman, but at five foot seven, she wasn't light as a feather. Letting out an exasperated breath, she almost sighed in relief when he swung her down so that he was carrying her in his arms. Sliding her arms around his neck, she decided to hang on to the ride until he finally let her down again. Then there would be hell to pay.

Chapter 8

When Killian stopped before a cabin, Brina was surprised, but she refused to speak. He didn't even let her down when he climbed up the steps. How far had he carried her? She looked over his shoulder and could have sworn she saw a pair of eyes watching from the bushes. Were they being followed by someone? Or something?

Killian balanced her with his knee as he turned the doorknob to push the door open. He carried her over to the fireplace that, strangely enough, was already burning. Had he been expecting company?

Killian let her feet slide to the floor. His hands touched her face and lifted it up slightly to look within her eyes, as if he were trying to see if she was inside. His thumb stroked her cheek and a softness covered his face. Brina thought he would kiss her, but he stepped away from her, turning his back on her completely.

Brina felt anger rise inside her. Why was he playing with

her? She wasn't a toy. She was a living, breathing woman, with feelings and apparently desire for men who constantly made jackasses out of themselves.

"Damn you, Killian," she muttered.

He turned at her words. Killian's eyes flashed hot as he stepped closer to her. "What was that, Brina?"

"I said damn you!"

At this point, his arms reached out for her, pulling her hard against him. His mouth was on hers before she uttered another word. She felt the low growl in his throat and she wrapped her arms around his neck. Pulling him in closer, Brina felt the anger growing. He was holding back; she could feel it. Just like last night, when he had basically pushed her aside. Pulling away from his kiss, she tried to catch her breath.

Her eyes met his again and they held her captive there. Brina barely noticed the fingers that pushed her jacket over her shoulders. The same fingers undid the snap of her jeans. Her stomach flinched when his hands slid against it. "What are you doing?"

Killian did not answer her. Instead, he pushed her jeans down her legs. His movements were slow and gentle, and he only broke eye contact with her for a few seconds. When his hands slid up her stomach, she realized her shirt was soon to follow. This was the second trance she had been in today. Brina tried to fight the foggy feeling that seeped into her bones, but this one was so much harder to fight. Every inch of her was screaming for him to follow through.

When he walked away from her, she blinked. Where was he going? How could he just leave her here like this? "Killian?"

Her eyes followed him across the room, where he retrieved a throw blanket from one of the couches. He moved closer to her and wrapped it around her. Then he left the room completely.

Brina stood there, realizing that he had stripped every inch of her down merely to cover her in a blanket. Not because he was about to have his wicked way with her at all, but because her entire body was cold and shivering. She slid to the floor before the fire and cursed him all up and down the eastern peninsulas. What had she done in her previous life to send her into her current reality? She pulled her knees against her and lay her head down on top of them as bitter tears fell down her face.

He had a vision of what he wanted for his life, Brina was sure of it. She simply didn't measure up to it. This knowledge shouldn't hurt her the way that it did. People came and people went. That was life. Brina had experienced that more times than she cared count. Yet here she was, feeling desperate for a stranger who really didn't want her.

When he came back into the room with a mug filled with something steamy, Brina refused to take it. "Leave me alone, Killian."

"Brina, take the damn drink." His words were curt, as if he refused to take no for an answer.

Brina reached for it and held it in her hands. She stared at the fire and tried to pretend he was nowhere near her, but even from a few feet away she could feel his heat against her.

"Drink."

Brina's lip curled up in anger as she took a small sip.

She swallowed it, wishing she could swallow the knot in her throat with it. From here, she could feel his anger rising.

"Look at me, Brina."

"*No.*"

It was a hollow whisper filled with defeat. She heard him growl and felt the anger rising in him, but she wasn't afraid of him. Killian would never hurt her. Her soul knew his, whether he admitted it or not. Even so, she was not about to make the same mistake in this lifetime. If they were meant to be together, it would have to wait until the next life, or maybe the one after that, depending on how much angrier he made her.

Killian slid down the floor next to her. His hand moved under her chin and slowly rotated her face to his. "Brina...."

"I hate you," she whispered as a tear slipped down her face.

"I know." He smoothed the tear away and sighed.

Brina jerked her head away from him. "Just go away."

"I can't." His voice was soft, yet somewhere in there was a hard edge.

Brina wasn't sure what that meant. He didn't want her, but he didn't want to leave her alone either? Anger started to spiral inside her. She let the blanket fall from her body and stood up above him, her hands on her hips and her breasts jutting out proudly before her. "I've never had a man make me feel so worthless. Am I that hideous to you?"

Gold flames flashed inside his eyes, and he was on his feet before Brina could protest. His mouth covered hers with a feverish pitch that robbed her senses from her head.

65

Brina's emotions bubbled up to the surface and she pushed him away. His breathing was ragged, as if he were trying to control himself. Brina felt much the same, but a raw bitterness was there between them.

"You can't keep doing this, Killian." Brina curled her hands into fists, her breasts heaving as she took deep angry breaths into her lungs.

"I want you, Brina." His teeth were clenched, as if he were trying to control something inside him.

"Oh? You could have fooled me." She crossed her arms over her chest and her chin jutted out proudly.

"I was a fool."

"Go on...." Brina waited to see if he would say something that would make her change her mind about him right in this moment.

A knock sounded at the door and Killian rolled his eyes angrily. "Son of a...."

Brina shook her head as she retrieved her wet clothes. "Maybe one of them can help me get back to the inn."

He pushed a hand through his hair. "Like hell. We're not done here."

"Speak for yourself," she bit out at him as he walked away. Wrapping the blanket around her, she took her clothes with her as she went in search of a bathroom. The more she felt her clothing, the more she knew walking around in them wouldn't be very wise. Especially since she didn't know where she was, or how long it would take to get back to her things. She settled for hanging them over a shower door before she went to see what else she might be able to find.

The cabin was actually quite functional. From the outside she would never have guessed how much space was inside it. It was actually two stories. Walking down the hall, she found stairs that led up and she took them. When she made it to the top, she found three doors.

"Hmm...if I were clothes, where would I be?" Brina went to the only room on the left side. If she had to guess, this was the master bedroom.

Pushing open the door, she saw that her assumption was correct. She walked over to the closet and looked inside it. She found a few T-shirts hanging inside and pulled one out. Brina was sure that whoever they belonged to would forgive her later. There was a pair of sweatpants folded on a shelf that looked like they would be a few sizes too large for her, but she pulled them out too. Sliding them over her legs, Brina tightened the strings so they wouldn't fall down her waist. The T-shirt hung low over her knees when she slid it over her head.

When she was done, Brina took a look around her. She felt like she knew every inch of this room, even though she had never been inside it before. From the small pictures on the tables, to the afghans that were folded over the side of the bed, the room had an essence about it — thoughtful, reserved. A wooden rocking chair stood just by the only window that let light inside it. It was well worn and aged from the countless hours its owner had sat glancing out the window, watching the world outside.

She reached out to stroke the wood. "*Killian.*"

Had he made this? It reminded her of some of the furniture

she had seen at Knight's Orchard. Whoever had made it had put every inch of themselves into the artistry. Brina couldn't resist the urge to sit down in it. She closed her eyes as the rocker moved effortlessly. Well made, like every inch of him. Brina opened her eyes and looked out the window. She saw Killian arguing with two of his brothers. Karter looked up at her, and gave a small nod and a smile. "Crap." Brina slid further back in the chair, but not far enough to miss seeing Killian look up at her. Even from here she could see the brooding on his face. He turned to his brothers and started gesturing at them like a mad man. She shook her head. "Bri, just what have you gotten yourself into?"

She saw Killian walk away with them and wondered when he might be back. She eyed his bed and yawned. Not having slept so well the night before, exhaustion was slowly working its way into her bones. Brina pushed up from the chair and walked over to the king-size bed.

"Wonder how many people you've squeezed in here." She smirked as naughty images filled her head. He could pull it off — he was certainly handsome enough. Pulling the covers up, she slid inside them and pulled them around her. When she put her head against the pillow, she sighed as his scent tickled her senses. Brina hugged the pillow closer to her and closed her eyes.

Whatever they had to talk about could wait, especially considering he had left her standing there vulnerable once more. Brina wondered if he would ever get it right, or if she would stick around to even let him try. For now, she would rest. Thinking could come later.

Chapter 9

When Brina woke, the room was dark. She was surprised to find she had slept the afternoon away. Had she really been that exhausted? Stretching quietly, her hands bumped into a solid object.

"Killian?" she whispered.

His drowsy voice answered. "Yes?"

"What are you doing?" Her heart was racing in her chest.

"Sleeping. Or I was," he answered ruefully.

"Here?" Her voice was almost accusing.

"Well, you *are* in my bed, Brina. Where else am I supposed to sleep?"

"Oh." She slid out the other side of the bed and looked for anywhere to retreat to.

"You didn't have to leave."

Brina could see the white of his teeth from here, even without the lights on. "Killian...."

"Sleep, Brina. Just sleep."

"I can't."

He pushed up from the bed and let out a loud sigh. "My presence bothers you that much?"

"No," she denied, because honestly, her anger was starting to subside a little. Perhaps having a little sleep had helped with that. Or the fact that the man had saved her from peril with little thought to his own safety. Then he had carried her away. Granted, he hadn't really given her a choice, but somehow, she knew his heart was in the right place.

"Then what is it?"

"I'm hungry. And if you must know, I have to pee."

Killian chuckled loudly. "Okay, you take care of the second one. I'll bring you some food."

"Can I have some tea too?" She asked him. Brina had only had a little of it earlier, but what she had was delicious.

"Anything," he answered her.

Anything? Really? Just how far did she want to push her luck? "Uh...."

"Yes, Brina?"

"Where is the bathroom up here?" She hadn't gotten that far.

Killian flung the blankets off him and Brina sucked in her breath. He wasn't naked, not entirely, but he might as well have been. Her eyes followed him as he walked across the room. Killian opened one of the doors and turned on the lights. "Master bath is right here."

"Oh." Now that the lights were surrounding him, her heart beat faster in her chest. She gulped slightly. He was the one with an animal inside, but she was the one who felt like devouring every inch of him. Her eyes met his and she saw the same light that always seemed to catch in them when he was studying her intently.

"What are you hungry for?" He asked her softly.

"Excuse me?" she almost squeaked. What was he talking about again?

"Food, Brina. What do you want to eat?" He was clearly amused.

"Oh. Right. A sandwich? Anything really. I'm not picky." No, she wasn't, but looking at him she realized she should have been much pickier in her partners before this moment. Compared to Killian, they were all duds. She moved closer to him and walked around him. Closing the door behind her, she tried to slow the beat of her heart. This time she knew he was chuckling when he walked away from the door. Damn him.

When she was done, Brina walked downstairs to help make the food. By the time she made it down the stairs, she realized that she had no idea where the kitchen was. When she had come in earlier, she had only seen the large living space with the couches and followed the hallway that led to the stairs. Walking through the living room, she heard the small sounds of a knife chopping something. She followed it through what must be the dining room.

Looking through the door connecting it, she saw Killian's back. So much strength as the muscles rippled under the lights, yet something else too. A deep weight. He carried a lot within him. For whatever reason, Brina wanted to lighten the load. She walked slowly across the floor and put her hands on him. He flinched under her touch, but relaxed when she slid her arms around him. Brina rested her head against him, knowing that if she spent a hundred nights doing just this very thing, it would never be enough.

"Almost done." Killian slid something onto the plate and pushed it aside.

Brina rubbed her hands along his stomach and felt him stiffen against her. "Relax, Killian, I'm not going to molest you."

Brina moved away from him and put her hands on the counter of the sink. How was this ever going to work? His wolf wanted her, but did he? Brina just had herself to contend with—maybe that's why it was easier for her. The only internal conflict she had was with herself. Like, why was she throwing herself at a man who didn't really know what he wanted? Didn't she deserve better? And yet, when she looked at him, she only wanted one thing.

She let out a loud sigh. "I'm sorry."

"Sorry?" Killian turned to face her, confusion on his face as he handed her a plate.

"It must be hard for you." Her eyes met his.

"How so?" His jaw seemed to harden as he waited for her answer.

"To want something different than the wolf inside you," she answered.

"What do you mean?" His jaw relaxed and his eyes softened.

"He thinks he wants me, but you don't. The two of you are at odds." Brina's eyes broke away from his.

"Is that what you think?" His voice was soft, almost inaudible.

Brina couldn't answer right away. To say it aloud only seemed to oversimplify the complicated way she felt about him. After a brief pause, she whispered, "Yes."

He never answered her. Instead, he took her hand and led her to the dining room. "Sit, Brina. Eat."

She did so, not because she wanted to be ordered around by him, but because her stomach started to rumble noticeably. The second she started to eat the sandwich, her whole body seemed to relax. When he brought her a hot cup of tea, she gave him a half-smile that seemed to appease him.

Though he joined her at the table, Brina noticed he didn't touch the food on his plate. "Aren't you hungry?"

"Yes," he answered.

"Why aren't you eating? Have I upset you?" Guilt rushed through her. As angry as she had been with him earlier, a switch had been turned on in her that she couldn't seem to shut off. Perhaps it was the empath in her. Before she had only been able to feel her own emotions, because she had shut that part of her brain off. But when she was tired and hungry, she had even less control over that. Killian was disturbed, but the exact emotion she couldn't quite put her finger on.

"Because I don't want food." His eyes flashed again and Brina looked away.

"What do you want, Killian?" She whispered across the void that seemed to be creeping up between them.

"*You.*"

Brina looked up at him. "You want me, or he wants me?"

73

"We're the same, Brina. What he wants, so do I."

"If you both want the same and he wants me, why do you push me away?" She asked him outright.

"Because this isn't something you should jump into lightly," he cautioned her.

"What, like I sleep around?" She crossed her arms over her chest.

Killian's fist slammed on the table. "That's not what I said."

"It seemed implied," she pointed out.

"I meant what I said, Brina. I can only have one mate. If you chose me, you would forsake all others. If you strayed…."

"What would happen, Killian?" She challenged him.

"I'd kill him." An anger seemed to explode across his face.

Brina laughed at him. The idea of her ever choosing another man over him was ridiculous to her. Although, having him toss some guy over in a rampage would be something worth seeing. The very thought of him wild and reckless over her made her blood boil slightly.

"You think I'm kidding, Brina. He already wants to hurt my brothers, and I'm half-tempted to help him." Killian ground his fist into his hands.

"Well, I couldn't have that." Brina reached over to touch his hands, but he jerked them away like he was on fire. He wanted her, but he didn't.

She picked up her plate and carried it to the sink. She found her shoes by the door and slid them on, not caring if he were behind her or not.

Brina opened the door and walked out into the crisp cool

air. She shut the door behind her and walked down the steps. Rubbing her arms, she shivered. A little cold wasn't going to stop her though. She needed space from him, especially if she were going to keep him from bruising her heart any further. He thought he was protecting her, but really, he was just protecting himself.

She had no idea where she was going, only that she needed space. The world seemed smaller whenever she was near him, the air harder to breathe. He represented everything she wanted, yet he was afraid to give it to her, as if it was a hardship she wouldn't be able to handle. Killian knew nothing about her, not really, which seemed odd, because the more she was around him the more she felt like she had known him her entire life. If he didn't feel that exact way, then what was he doing toying with her? The back and forth was going to drive her insane.

Heading into the woods, she let the energy around her lead her. The trees cast shadows on the ground as the moon glowed around her. Brina looked up at the sky and saw the shining orb. So much magic ebbed and flowed through its light, the same magic that flowed through Killian's veins. What he didn't realize was the same magic coursed through her. Maybe it didn't shift her into another creature, but it certainly made her unlike other girls.

Brina saw a large boulder in the middle of a small clearing that called to her. Walking over to it, she put her hand on it and felt a familiar tingle enter her hand. How often had he sat here? Did he look up at the moon and ponder the universe the way she did? Brina sat down and sighed. Her mother had always told her that when she found her love, she should hang onto it at all costs. What her mother had failed to tell her was that she might have to drag him kicking and screaming into it. Brina wasn't sure she had that kind of resolve, not when he treated her so carelessly. His touch, his taste, his smell, it all left her feeling wrecked inside.

A snap of a twig caught her attention. She didn't even bother to turn around. Brina knew he was there. Was it instinct, or did his pheromones emanate so much that every inch of her knew its scent?

"Killian?" She called to him. When he didn't answer, she turned to look into the line of trees. Brina didn't see the man; instead she saw the beast. She smiled at him and beckoned him closer with her hand. When he refused to move, Brina sighed. Pushing away from the rock, she made her way slowly to the beast that was watching her with wary eyes. He growled slightly, but Brina shook her head at him.

"I'm not afraid of you."

As she stood in front of him, Brina took in every inch of the wolf in front of her. His golden eyes held some of the hazel that had just begun to haunt her dreams. His grey fur was filled with black accents that ran up from his black nose. Kneeling down, she reached out to touch him. The wolf pulled away from her, but Brina refused to give up. She sat down on the ground next to him and waited for him to make the next step.

When the wolf laid its head on her shoulder, Brina sighed against him. "It's a beautiful night." Brina knew he wouldn't answer her, but he did step even closer to her. She wrapped her arm around his neck. "Almost peaceful."

The closer the wolf got to her, the easier it was to feel the heartbeat in his chest. So much like Killian's heart. The two were one, even though they seemed so separate. She shivered slightly as a breeze blew against her. The wolf nuzzled her head and she smiled. He was far more affectionate than the male part of him.

Brina turned to look in his eyes and ran her hand along his snout, and his tongue snaked out to lick her. Brina giggled. "That tickles."

Heat flashed in the wolf's eyes and Brina pulled away slowly. She rose from the ground and brushed herself off. Brina started to make her way back through the woods, but his voice called to her.

"Brina."

She felt the need dripping in it, but she was afraid to look at him. Not because of what he might look like after transforming, but because she couldn't handle rejection from him one more time. Brina put one foot in front of the other, ignoring the need to look at him. Had she not humiliated herself enough? Let him burn for a change.

Chapter 10

When she opened the door, she didn't hear Killian enter behind her. His arms wrapped around her stomach and pulled her against him. She felt his breath on her neck and she shivered. Closing her eyes, she tried not to let his nearness distract her. She had been here before, and each time she had been left wanting something he was afraid to give her.

His mouth kissed her neck as his hands ran along her stomach. Brina's breath caught in her throat when his teeth bit her ear lobe. "I want you, Brina."

She sighed against him when his fingers started to massage her hips. One of his hands moved under her shirt and started its journey upward, where it rubbed against one of her nipples. She whimpered against him.

"If I go much further...." His ragged breath was her sign that he was trying to rein in his desire for her. His mouth continued to tease the base of her neck as his fingers tweaked over the other nipple. Brina was almost a puddle at his feet.

"It can't be undone." Hot air on her earlobe again — Brina thought she was going to fall over on the spot.

Arching into him, her stomach tightened when his other hand ran along it. *"Please."*

He growled against her neck as he bit it softly. "Please what, Brina? You have to say it."

Brina turned in his arms and pulled his face down so that she could look him in the eyes. She didn't want there to be any way he could misinterpret her words. "Make me yours, Killian."

"You're sure?" He asked her one last time.

"I think I might die if you deny me," she pouted up at him.

A slow grin slid across his face right before he scooped her up in his arms and started to carry her up the stairs.

"Killian, I am capable of walking."

He refused to answer her. Instead, he kept his eyes focused on the task at hand. When he kicked open his door, Brina giggled. When her eyes met his, she realized it wasn't a laughing matter at all. Killian had a very serious look plastered on his face. She wondered what was going through his head. When he let her feet slide to the floor, Brina looked up at him again. She ran her hand across his face and sucked in her breath when he moved his mouth to kiss her palm. Had it always been that sensitive?

"Killian?"

"Yes, Brina."

"I...." What did she want to tell him? The more she looked in his eyes, the harder it was to remember. "You should know

I'm not about to give up my work."

"Fine." He nibbled on her hand and her insides quivered.

"I'm a pain to get along with."

"I have four brothers—it can't be worse than that." He grinned at her before licking her finger.

"What if you change your mind?" Brina knew she was sure, but she didn't want to ruin his life. "You'd be stuck with me."

He ran his hand through her hair. "Brina...."

"Yes?" She almost stopped breathing, waiting for his reply.

"Stop talking."

"But—"

The rest of her words were put to rest as his mouth covered hers. She wrapped her arms around his neck and savored the feel of his kiss. His fingers worked at the ties of the sweatpants. When he loosened them, they fell to the floor with little effort. He stood back to look at her. "I'll never look at that shirt the same."

Brina blushed and fidgeted with the bottom hem. She bit her bottom lip and looked up at him. His eyes flashed, and she understood that it was the way beast merged with man and man merged with beast. It was their desire to make her theirs, to mark her for life.

"Too bad it's in the way." He moved toward her, his stealth sexy and dangerous at the same time, but he didn't frighten her.

His hands pushed the shirt up over her head, and she stood naked before him for the second time that day. Brina felt a shyness now that she hadn't felt earlier. Would she be enough for him? To her, Brina's body was average. Perhaps curvier than most other women, but she hid it well under her clothing.

Killian pulled her tight against him, his hands molding her behind like a sculptor as his mouth took her in. When his tongue slid inside her mouth, she sighed against him. His taste, his touch, they both wrapped around her like a hazy concerto with a rising pitch that echoed in every inch of her. She felt his erection warm against her leg, and realized that somewhere along the line he had lost his clothing too. Brina wanted to stand back and take in his beautiful body, but Killian was slowly edging her back to the bed.

When he lowered her back against it, she shivered against the heat of his body as excitement started to rise within her.

His eyes met hers. "Brina."

"Yes, Killian?"

"It's going to hurt," he tried to warn her.

"You're not that big. I mean, you are...."

Killian burst out laughing and started to hoot just a little. "You are precious, Brina."

"Now you're making fun of me," she pouted.

"It's not the actual mating that makes you mine, Brina. Although it is part of it."

Brina understood that. Sex could be tantric. Many rituals called for it, none that she been a part of before. She bit her lip and tried to ask the next question without sounding naive. "What happens?"

"I have to bite you."

"Oh." She shivered slightly and her eyes met his. "Okay."

"Not yet. It will be easier if you aren't thinking about it."

"Well, that's going to be hard considering how it's the only thing I'm thinking of right now." She punched him playfully on the shoulder.

His mouth covered hers and his tongue plunged inside. He readjusted his body so that he was lying next to her. Her body mourned the loss of his heat. Killian continued to kiss her as his hand found the small nest of curls between her legs.

When his finger slid against her clit, Brina broke the kiss. "What are you...?"

"Relax, Brina," he whispered into her ear.

She tried her best to follow his order, but the fire he was stirring with his fingers was hard to ignore. Something grew inside her, a feeling that had been long dormant. Her stomach fluttered as her body started to climb for something just out of reach. Her breath caught in her throat as something pooled in her loins. She was just on the edge of something she hadn't felt in quite some time, if ever.

"That's it, Brina." The hot on her ears, the soft gruff whisper, the way his fingers moved against her silky core, it all drove her well past her breaking point. When the orgasm shook through her, she couldn't breathe. She thought his movements would still, but he continued to drive her further. She was well past the point of no return when an even stronger desire ripped through her.

"Come on, Bri. That's it."

No one had ever called her that, except for herself when she was talking to herself. She liked the way it sounded, especially when he whispered it against her ear. Her stomach clenched tightly as a wave of pleasure and pain tried to send her to oblivion. The more his fingers moved, the harder it was to deny the craziness racing through her. When her body shook against his hand, Killian's teeth sunk into her neck.

"Oh!" she shouted as the combination of pleasure and pain rippled through her again. His fingers never stopped working their magic as his mouth tried to soothe the wound at her neck. Her eyelids felt heavy with desire as he wove his own spell around her. The magic of the moment wasn't lost on her.

He moved over her and held her face in front of his. "Are you all right, Bri?"

"No," she whispered.

His eyes were filled with concern. "Did I hurt you?"

"Yes," she whispered.

"Where does it hurt?" His mouth kissed her cheek.

"I ache for you, Killian." She pulled his mouth down to hers and drank him in. She felt the tension drain from his shoulders as his tongue dueled with her own.

When he broke the kiss, his eyes were almost reckless. "I can't wait much longer, Bri."

"Then don't." She gave him a sexy smile and waited for him to respond.

He didn't disappoint her. Killian spread her legs and slid his cock deep inside her. His heat filled her to the core. Brina met every thrust with her hips, the fire burning inside her. As he picked up the pace, she felt a small flutter inside her as her desire rose higher and higher. The faster he went, the more she wanted, until the world seemed to spin around her. White lights exploded behind her eyes as she came undone.

He growled when she came against him, and the beast inside seemed to take over as his hips ground against hers. Faster he pushed, harder, until he stretched her to the core. Brina enjoyed every wicked moment as he came crashing into her. She saw his neck straining as he found his finish. Her insides pulled him in as they quivered around him one last time.

When he was finished, he rolled away from her and tried to catch his breath. Killian pulled her against him and kissed the top of her head.

Brina sighed against him. She liked the feel of his skin on hers. Her insides were still throbbing. Closing her eyes, she tried to still the racing of her heart.

"Did I hurt you?" His voice was filled with concern.

"What?" she blinked. What was he talking about?

His hand moved over her neck and she flinched slightly. Had he bit her? His mouth kissed her neck, and his tongue moved over her wound. Her breath caught in her throat.

"Mmmm...."

"Sleep, Bri."

She yawned as if on command and snuggled against him. "I'm a lucky woman."

"Why's that?" he asked her softly.

"Because I get you both."

Killian growled as he pulled her closer to him. "Forget him. You're all mine."

"Good, and don't you forget it."

"Never."

He kissed her softly one last time, then pulled her closer to him. His hand stroked her head as she fell asleep beside him, feeling safer than she had her entire life.

Chapter 11

When Brina awoke later, the room was filled with darkness. The moon's glow barely filtered into the room through the window. She sighed as she stretched. Her muscles were a little sore, as if she'd run a marathon, but she didn't care. It had been worth every delicious moment.

"Killian?" she whispered. Turning over, she found the bed was completely empty.

Where had he gone to? She slid out of the bed and retrieved the clothes she had worn earlier. As she walked down the stairs, she thought she'd find him sitting in the living room, but he wasn't there either. After checking the entire house, it was clear Killian had left. She went to the hallway closet and found a warm coat inside it. Sliding it on, she zipped it up around her and sighed as his scent filtered through her nose. Closing her eyes, she imagined it was his arms wrapped around her right now, keeping her warm.

She retrieved her shoes and slid them over her feet.

When she was done, Brina opened the door and stepped out into the cold night air. Scanning the world around her, she felt something pulling her from across the woods. It wasn't Killian, neither was it the voice that had transfixed her earlier.

It was the magic of a light worker. She recognized the peaceful flow of energy that offered a calm to the world around it, perhaps building up to the full moon. Sometimes they held their rituals from days before until the moon was round in the sky. Then the witches would release their light into the world to heal the rift between time and space. They had their hands full with the vitriol that fueled the world these days.

Brina sighed. She didn't understand how some people lived their lives hating anything that wasn't like them — race, religion, creed, nationality. There was a serious lack of love in the world. People didn't seem to have a right to their beliefs. It was always the loudest voice that crammed the others down deep back into the earth.

A lone howl sent a shiver down her spine, and it wasn't fear that quivered through her. "Killian."

When a series of howls followed, she realized he was out with his pack. She wondered why they were out right now. Had they felt the magic too? Brina was drawn to it, but now that her brain seemed to be functioning properly, she decided to not let it overrun her thoughts. No more chasing after disembodied voices, not without having back up.

The voice that had taken her over earlier, she could not place it. The phenomena wasn't something she'd experienced before. Was it demonic? Sometimes demons would take over people, possess them to override the good inside them. Evil fed on the light, as it manipulated it. She wasn't sure it wanted to manipulate her or steal her soul.

But, what good would it do for a demon to send her to her death in the river? It would get far more power from her if it were able to use her soul as fuel while she was still alive. They would drain the light slowly until nothing remained, then they would cast their host aside. This had to be something or someone else. Someone with the ability to manipulate the unsuspecting. Brina wondered if that was why she had been sent here.

How many witches had lost their lives in that river? That was something she would need to look into. Maybe Killian and his brothers would know. Did they prowl the woods nightly? If so, chances were they knew more about this area than she had first thought. Brina made a mental note to ask Killian in the morning. That was, if she weren't distracted by his handsome face. She could gaze into his eyes for eternity and never get bored with the view.

As Brina made her way through the woods, she bent some of the plants at her feet to mark her way home. This time she refused to get lost inside the forest. She walked until she saw a light glow breaking through the line of trees. Stopping before they broke, she peered around a large tree to see what the source was, and breathed a sigh of relief when she saw a lone witch beside a large fire.

"Come on out," the witched called to her.

Brina stepped around the tree and held up a hand. "I come in peace."

"Only a friend may enter the circle, if you care to risk it."

The woman was several years older than her. Her long brown hair flowed down her shoulders, with faded strands of white marking her age.

Brina nodded to her and said a small silent blessing before stepping into the circle that was clearly marked with the four small stones that were placed around the fire. The four corners, north, east, south, and west, represented the elements that breathed life into the world around them. "Merry meet," Brina greeted her. "I'm —"

"I know who you are, Ms. Moss." Her eyes looked her up and down, sizing her up without a second thought. "I know why you are here."

"And you are?"

"Marina. I protect these woods from *him*." Her words were soft on the breeze.

"Are there others?" Brina asked her.

"They are afraid to come out at night. It's no longer safe for us here." Marina looked down to the ground sadly.

"Who is he?" Brina wasn't surprised to hear there was a male involved. Could it be the same man who had taken her over earlier?

"We don't know. We only feel his energy. He is angry at the world. And at us." Marina threw some herbs into the fire and they shot up a few feet higher.

"Can he be stopped?"

"If his power source is removed. We don't believe he is a man of magic, not a true one at least. There are many that think they can control the elements at their whim. They do not realize the elements work through us, not the other way around. We are at their mercy."

"Magic is often like that," agreed Brina. "How many have been lost?"

"Ten over the last two years. One a month for the past three. He grows hungrier, but for what, I just don't know." Marina looked at her and their eyes met. "They brought you here."

"Yes. Their spirits called to me."

"Then maybe you can help them find their final resting place." Marina reached into the pocket of her robes. She held open her hand and revealed a crystal quartz. "For you, to keep you protected from his spell. I fear you may need it."

"He's already targeted me." Brina now understood that the man behind this was exceptionally dangerous. She would have to tread very carefully. Stepping closer to Marina, she accepted her gift. "Has the local law enforcement been helpful?"

"Not really. When the bodies were retrieved from the water, they ruled it as accidental drowning. You and I both know there was nothing accidental about it." Marina's face contorted in disgust. "You've been marked," the witch commented as she pointed to her neck.

Brina touched her hand to her neck and felt the welts forming beneath her fingertips. "Oh. Yes. I—"

"It's about time he took a mate." Marina smiled at her. "I think he's chosen well."

"You know Killian?" Brina was almost surprised.

"We know all of them. The Knight pack helps keep our woods safe, as much as they can. They have kept many of us from succumbing to the darkness here. We're indebted to them." Marina waved her hands and the fire changed color. Blue flames flickered among the yellow. "The magic is strong in those wolves. The light flows through their veins."

Brina didn't really need her to tell her that. She could sense the good in him, no matter how cruel he had seemed to her before. Brina knew that he was trying to protect her even then. The only problem she had with it now was that he would have to learn she was capable of taking care of herself—most of the time. When she wasn't distracted, that was. Today, that had been the first time any negative energy had been able to take over her thoughts. Brina would make sure it never happened again.

"Do you live near here?" Brina asked her curiously.

"On the outskirts of Witch's Hollow in the small encampment there. There are several of us there. If you bring that necklace with you, all will recognize you as friend. Although, when some of them find out you have mated with Killian, they may not be too happy."

"Oh?"

"Quite a few of them are smitten with him. There are at least two that had hoped he would make them his mate."

Two women? Had he known them intimately? Had he slept with them? Brina wasn't sure she could face off with them, but even if she did, it wouldn't change the outcome. No matter how much they fought against it, Killian was hers. This wasn't something that could be reversed. That wasn't how it worked. One mate for life. She would face them with her head held high, for he had chosen her.

"Well, they can't have him." Her chin jutted out proudly before her.

"Good girl. They won't make it easy for you," she cautioned her.

"I'm not afraid of them." Brina opened her hands and created a small ball of light. "I can protect myself."

Marina chuckled. "That you can. You are stronger than you know, even stronger now that you have mixed your soul with his. You'll need his help if you're going to put the darkness here to rest."

"Understood, but I'll probably leave him home if I visit the camp." Brina smiled ruefully.

"Bring him. I could use a good laugh." Marina's eyes twinkled merrily.

Brina had the distinct impression that Marina liked to stir the pot just a bit. She liked the old woman's spunk.

Brina heard the sound of movement around them. Turning to the sound, she saw the imp that had attacked her the night before. Her hands clenched in reflex and static electricity fluttered between her fingers.

"Relax, he can't attack you inside the circle," reminded Marina. "Or do you not trust the power of the circle?"

She lowered her hands. "Of course, I do. Who does that belong to?"

"The dark casters. He's harmless really. Just watches the night and reports back to them."

"Well, he sure had a story to tell last night," Brina grinned.

"He usually does." Marina winked at her. "But for tonight, I think the news of your joining will be enough to keep his masters entertained."

Brina blushed. She hadn't realized that their business would be broadcast all over the area. Some things should remain private. She looked down at the ground and closed her eyes.

"Don't worry. They won't mind. They may stir up the darkness around us, but they don't do anything to undo the balance. Too much light can never survive without its dark counterpart."

"So, the black magic isn't something to fear here?"

"Only fear black magic when that's all there is, child. You should know that by now. Your mother taught you well, as did you grandmother," Marina reminded her.

"They did." This wasn't the first time a witch had recognized her lineage. Pedigree was often something that was easy to read, like an extra lining to her aura that reverberated around her. Brina could see the magic that circled around Marina as well, who was a Dianic witch if she wasn't mistaken.

"That will serve you well. Witches always make the best mates. That's probably why their father chose Amber." She smiled as she mentioned Killian's mother.

"She's a witch?" How had she missed that earlier? That wasn't like her. Had Brina been too pre-occupied with the spell Killian had already started to weave over her?

"She is a solitary, and hides her energy well. Mark my words, though, she's not one to push aside. Her love for her flock is strong."

"I can see that." And she could. Amber Knight had a strong

personality, one that had seemed at odds with her own. Brina hadn't even thought about how their joining would affect the rest of his family. She knew she would have to face the music sooner rather than later.

She turned to find the imp scampering off, feeling slightly awkward for having assumed he was a danger to her before. The dark of night could play tricks on people though. Maybe it was Killian that she had felt, the danger of being near him. Not that he was dangerous, but the feelings that had risen so close to the surface.

A howl shattered the silence, and Brina's breath caught in her throat as the hair stood on the back of her neck. She sighed as she heard the beauty in it.

"He's calling for you." The witch waved her arms to the east.

"I know." She smiled at her. "Merry meet, and merry part, Marina. I promise to do my best to find this man who is decimating your ranks."

"I know you will. That's why the spirits chose you. Now, run along. Can't keep a beast waiting." She winked at her.

Brina tried to fight the blush rising to her face. She bowed her head and stepped back from the circle. Having learned all she could from Marina at the moment, she let her heart lead her through the forest, searching for the lonely howl that serenaded her soul.

Chapter 12

The lonely howls led her through the wilderness, deeper into the darkness, but Brina wasn't afraid of it. She knew that Killian would keep her safe. When she got closer to him, she could sense his presence. It was like a calm wind that wrapped itself around her. When she saw him standing six feet ahead of her, the wolf nodded to her.

Brina smiled at him and sat down on the ground. She waited for him to make his way over to her, and wasn't disappointed when the wolf trotted over to her. He put his head on her shoulder and Brina wrapped her arms around him. She felt the gentle hum of energy flow between them. Closing her eyes, she sighed. "I missed you."

I missed you too.

Brina blinked. Had she just heard his voice? Pulling back from him, she looked inside his eyes. "Killian?"

Yes, Bri.

"I didn't know you could speak like this." A smile lit up

ELISSA DAYE

her face as she lowered her head to his. She rubbed her nose against his.

After joining, my soul can communicate wherever you are.

"So, if I call for you?"

I will always hear you.

Brina liked the sound of that. "Good."

His wolf form moved a few steps away. It contorted slightly as the fur was retracted. Brina watched in awe as the wolf shifted into the warm-blooded man she had come to know so well. The process looked painful, as his skin stretched over the length of him. When he was done, he lay crouching on the ground. Brina found it curious that he wasn't completely naked—he was wearing a pair of jeans. How that worked she wasn't entirely sure, but some things were beyond explanation.

His hazel eyes watched her, to see if she would be disgusted by the mutation. When she didn't speak, his voice whispered across the void between them. "Brina?"

Tears filled her eyes as she moved closer to him. *"Killian."*

"I don't have to shift around you," he whispered as he pulled her into his arms. "If it scares you."

Brina put a hand on his face and stroked it. "I'm not afraid of it, Killian."

"Then why are you crying?" he asked her.

"Because I don't like to see you in pain." She kissed his cheek and snuggled against him.

His voice was gruff when he answered. "It's not all that bad."

"Liar," she whispered as she stroked her hand over his

neck.

A slow rumble erupted from his chest as he laughed. "Woman, what am I going to do with you?"

Their eyes met and Brina licked her lips. "Whatever you want, I hope."

The heat erupted in his eyes as her words sunk in. His mouth was on hers before she could utter another word. Her heart beat in her chest to a rhythm that matched his beside her. Their souls aligned together in that moment.

"As much as I'd like to take you outside in the moonlight, I fear we have spectators." He glanced out at the tree line.

"Your brothers?"

"Voyeurs...the lot of them." He shook his head ruefully. "Remind me to kill them later."

Brina giggled. "No way. I might need them to hold you back."

"Why's that?"

"Someday I'm going to make you angry." She smiled knowingly. Brina wasn't a fool. She knew she was hard to live with. Sometimes she had trouble living with herself.

"I would never hurt you, Brina." His hand stroked her cheek.

"You say that now." She grinned at him. "Give it time."

"Minx." He teased her right before he kissed her again. His hand caressed the mark on her neck, the one symbol that had united them. When he pulled away from her, he stood up and offered his hand. "Let's go home."

Home. She liked the sound of that. Brina had been a perpetual roamer, chasing one thing after another. The need to save those that were being hunted filled her to the core. She didn't think she could give that up any time soon. Her work was far too important.

She held his hand as they walked in silence through the dark forest. Glancing down, she found he was leading her back by the path she had marked earlier. She couldn't help wondering how long it would take her to memorize the woods before her, especially when all the trees seemed to look the same.

By the time they made it back to the cabin, she wondered if his desire for her had fizzled out. Besides holding her hand, he had made no other advances toward her. That was a shame really. She rather liked the idea of him having his wicked way with her out in the open. Not that she wanted his family to watch, though. She'd never be able to look at them again.

The minute the door closed behind them, Brina could sense the shift in him. She didn't even have to turn around to see it. The pulse between them beat erratically, and she shivered in expectation. She unzipped the coat and walked to the closet to hang it up. Brina barely closed the door before Killian pulled her into his arms. The breath almost left her lungs as excitement raced through her. His mouth closed on hers and she almost purred.

His fingers pulled the strings at her waist, and when he couldn't undo the knot, a loud rip sounded as he tore the material. She felt long nails, almost like claws, as they scraped her skin gently. She shivered against him as his hands moved behind her and pulled her tighter against him. As they pushed up her back, she realized he was completing his task.

She raised her arms and let him remove her shirt. He broke the kiss long enough to remove it before he devoured her lips.

Brina arched into him and felt his skin run along her breasts. She whimpered slightly when her nipples ran across his muscled flesh. Her hand slid between them and worked on the button of his jeans. When she slid the zipper down, his stomach seemed to ripple in anticipation.

Her other hand slid down, and she pushed his jeans over his hips. When they slid to the floor, her hand reached down and wrapped around his erection.

Killian growled against her. He broke the kiss and pulled her head back by her hair as he made a path of fire down her neck. Brina squeezed him hard and was rewarded with a sharp bite.

"You drive me wild, Brina," he whispered into her ear before licking her lobe.

Her nails raked against his cock lightly as a need coursed through her. "Same."

"You're playing with fire, Brina," he warned her.

"You don't scare me, Killian." She squeezed him as hard as she could and felt his stomach bunch up in reflex. She licked her lips. "I always liked fire."

He trembled before her. "If you push me too far...."

"Oh?" Brina smirked at him as she leaned up to kiss him. When his mouth came down to hers, she pulled just out of his reach. Desire flashed in his eyes, the same feeling swirling deliciously through her. She was in control of the beast and the man. Both were entranced by her, and she felt power coursing through her at that knowledge.

"It's my turn, Killian," she whispered to him as she ran kisses down his face. Her hands stroked him slowly as she made her way down his belly, alternating with hot kisses and painful bites that made him flinch beneath her. When she made it to her knees, she looked up at him and licked her lips.

"What are you...? Ohhhh...," he moaned when she took his cock into her mouth.

Brina had never felt the need to take a man into her like this before. She had never known the pleasure of having a man completely under her spell. Every time she pulled him in deeper, he groaned. When she bit against him, his legs trembled beneath him. She felt the heady power of control race through her as she reached for his scrotum. Squeezing him in her hands as she sucked him hard into her mouth, Brina felt a ripple of fire race through her. His hips started to grind as he moved himself deeper into her mouth. She drove him to the brink, until he pushed her face away from him.

"Witch," he accused her.

She licked her lips and smiled. "Don't you forget it." She rose and put her hands on her hips. Her breasts jutted out proudly as she seemed to taunt him. "What are you going to do about it?"

Another flash of gold and he growled low in his chest. When he picked her up, Brina wrapped her arms and legs around him. His cock slid into her and she gasped aloud. "Oh!"

"Hold on, Brina," he ordered her as his hips started to move.

Her breath caught in her throat as he pumped into her.

His balance was strong as his hands grabbed her ass for better leverage. She burned for him as his heat seared her. Her hands reached for his face and pulled him into a kiss. Their tongues dueled for control as he stroked deep inside of her. Brina started to move against him, riding him as the fire ignited inside her. She shook around him as her climax ripped through her. His wasn't far behind.

His voice almost sounded like a howl when he came inside her. "Yes! God yes. Bri...."

She trembled in his arms, still connected to him in the most intimate way. She lay her head against his shoulder and sighed softly. "That was...."

He kissed the top of her head, as no words could describe the way it was between them. When he carried her upstairs to bed, she found herself fading fast. Loving him was exhausting. She hoped it always remained that way. When he wrapped his arms around her, Brina fell into a peaceful sleep with him by her side.

Chapter 13

The next morning, Brina was happy to find herself still snuggled in the strength of his arms. She sighed against him, at peace for the first time in a long time. Was this what she had been searching for all these years? No other man measured up to the one whose heart beat next to hers. They were one, the two of them. Well, three, if she added his wolf into the equation—a wolf who seemed even gentler than the man, which was an irony in itself.

His mouth kissed her shoulder. "Good morning, Bri."

She squeezed his arms closer around her. When his fingers stroked against her stomach her insides shook. "What are you doing, Killian?"

"Making love to *my* woman." His teeth nibbled against her skin and she shuddered.

"You're insatiable!" she accused him.

His finger thrummed against her nipple, which was already hard. "I'm not the only one."

When his other hand slid down her stomach, she clenched her legs together.

"Open for me, Bri."

His whisper sent a shiver down her spine. Her legs opened, giving him access to his target. His fingers worked slowly against her clit and a heat filled her core. His mouth rained small kisses along the base of her neck as he stroked her gently. His other hand continued to play with her breasts, one after the other.

Her insides quaked slowly as an intense need started to fill every inch of her body. It wasn't fair, the pull he had over her. It was downright dangerous. She could see many a battle forfeited to his touch, his taste, as he conquered her resolve.

"Oh," she moaned as the desire racing through her came to a peak. She climbed over it as his fingers stroked her faster. The building momentum inside her was almost painful as her body craved the finish line he was driving her to.

"Cum for me, Bri."

His words sent a shiver down her entire body, which was punctuated by the orgasm that shattered through her. He refused to let her rest, as he picked up the pace. His hips pushed his erection into her back as he gyrated behind her. The knowledge that his desire for her was driving closer made her spiral even further out of control. She bucked against his cock as her body trembled painfully. She felt his teeth sink into her flesh, and she lost her mind as her desire took her over the edge of insanity.

She started to move against his fingers, riding the wave to the shores, only to push back for more. Brina was almost breathless, and when he shifted her hips, she whimpered her discontent. His hands pulled her legs further apart and he slid into her wet core. She moaned against him as he started to pump slowly into her.

"So wet for me. Oh, Bri." His fingers continued to work their magic as he moved in and out of her.

The lights exploded behind her eyes, like fireworks trickling down the sky. One right after another, he took every chance he could to make her cum against him, enjoying every second of her brutal need for him.

He continued to slide in and out of her with a hand on her breast, squeezing and massaging them tight, and one at her clit, giving her no quarter. Brina was ready to pass out in ecstasy. Killian was pushing her past all her limits. Every inch of her throbbed for whatever he gave her, and no matter how much of him she took in, she craved even more.

When she thought she could take no more, he pulled out of her, releasing her. She shivered when he removed his heat. She wondered what was happening, until his hands wrapped around her and flipped her onto her stomach. "What are you...?"

He manipulated her body so that she stood on all fours. Sliding her legs open wide, she felt his tongue slide against her clit. "Oh, my."

"You taste so good, Bri," he murmured as he bit the inside of her leg.

Bri jumped at the exquisite pleasure that he kept strumming inside her. His finger slid inside her as his tongue worked her over. She quivered in excitement. "Oh!"

He made her wild for him, mastering her with his touch. When he removed himself from her, Brina mourned the loss. She whimpered aloud, wanting so much more. His hand squeezed her ass seconds before he shoved himself inside of her. From this angle she seemed to take even more of him into her. His movements were jerking and fast, as the animal in him wanted to take over. He may not be shifted at the moment, but Brina could tell the difference. The wildness that took over him shook her to the core. His hands slid around her and squeezed her breasts as he took her from behind. She arched her back when his teeth bit her shoulder. Her orgasm was pain and pleasure, as his cock slammed into her over and over.

"That's right Bri, cum for me. Oh god, yes." His nails scratched her breasts as he squeezed them tight in his palms.

Brina ignored the pain and gyrated her hips to meet his every movement. She felt him stiffen behind her, and knew he was trying to prolong the moment. Brina was tempted to push him further and faster, but she was enjoying this far too much to want it to end.

He slowed his pace as if he were teasing himself, and Brina shook around him again. When he felt her orgasm again, a wild need seemed to take him over. His cock ravaged her silky core over and over, until neither of them could catch their breaths. She erupted around him just as his orgasm shook through him. Brina had never felt so close to any living being in her life as she did right then, with his cock still pulsing inside her. She shivered around him and he groaned.

"What you do to me."

"Mmmm...," she sighed when he moved slowly in and out of her until his erection no longer held and he pulled out of her.

Killian pulled her into his lap and kissed her softly on the lips. "I don't think I'll ever get enough of you."

"Good, 'cause you're stuck with me," she teased him.

"I'm not sure who got the short end of the stick with that one," he chuckled.

She punched him playfully on the shoulder. Brina put her hands on his face and pulled him down to a deeper kiss. She sighed against him when he broke the kiss.

"It's time to face the music, Bri," he warned her. His eyes were probing hers softly.

A tear formed in each eye. "What if she hates me?"

"My mother?" he asked her softly.

"*Yes.*" she whispered, and sniffled slightly.

"She'll respect my choice," assured Killian.

"What if —?"

Killian kissed her before she could ask another question. When she was nearly breathless, he removed his lips. "You think too much, Bri."

"A fault, I assure you. I tried to warn you." She really had tried to warn him, but he was too pig headed to listen.

"I'll just have to find ways to keep you distracted."

Her eyebrows rose curiously. "Oh?"

"Later, Bri. I brought your things." He gestured to the suitcase by the door.

When had he gotten those? Had his brothers helped him? She rubbed her hand across his cheek and smiled. "Thank you."

"You can thank me later." He winked at her.

"Promise?" She let her breasts tease his skin, and reveled in the tremor that shook through him.

"Bri...," he cautioned her.

"Your loss," she teased him as she pushed up from his lap. She walked over to the suitcase and pulled some clothes out for the day.

Killian was already pulling on clothes. "I'm going to make some coffee while you freshen up."

"Sounds good." She walked over to him and kissed him softly. "Thank you, Killian."

"For what?" His voice was soft.

"I've waited all my life for you." She sighed as his lips came down to hers again. When he broke the kiss, he put his head against hers.

"Get your shower, before he takes over," he warned her.

"Hardly. I think you're both pretty spent," she teased him before slapping his ass with her hand.

"Woman, don't try me." A golden light flashed in his eyes. "You're not getting out of brunch, Brina."

Her hopes deflated as he saw through her plan. "It was worth a try."

He chuckled against her. "Oh, you are going to keep me on my toes."

"Always." She tapped her finger on his nose and pushed away from him. She didn't bother to turn back around as she made her way into the bathroom.

Chapter 14

When Brina was done with her shower and dressed, she looked in the mirror. Her neck was just a little pink from where he had bitten her. She touched the mark gently and felt no pain. She closed her eyes as she remembered the first time their bodies had mated together. Brina hope it would forever be imprinted in her mind.

"Does it hurt?" His voice was quiet behind hers.

Brina turned around to look at him. "No."

"Are you sure?" His face was filled with guilt for causing her any ounce of pain.

Brina smiled up at him as her hand moved over the mark slowly. "I kinda like it. Gives me character."

Killian shook his head. "You're a conundrum."

"No more than you, sir!" She accused him playfully.

He handed her a cup of coffee. "I wasn't sure how you liked it, so I guessed."

She took a drink and found it light and sweet, the way she

preferred it. "It's perfect. Like you."

Killian leveled his eyes on her. "What are you up to, Bri?"

"What?" she asked innocently.

"Bri...."

"Fine. Do we *have* to go?" Not a single part of her wanted to leave this cabin, especially if it meant marching in to deal with the consequences of their joining. Amber Knight was not going to be pleased at all. She had sensed the woman's contempt for her the minute she sat next to her.

"You have nothing to be afraid of, Bri. My mother knows my choice."

Brina grimaced slightly at those words. She blushed as she realized every single one of them would know they had slept together. Looking down at the floor, her lips trembled slightly before she took another sip. Before she knew it, she had drained the cup. "Maybe just one more cup?"

"Liquid courage?" he teased her.

"Gearing up for the fight," she answered before she thought better of it. Her hand covered her mouth and she looked away from him.

"Bri, it's time to go," he told her. "If we put it off any longer, she'll come. Better to go there."

"Fine."

Brina shook her head and walked out of the room before she could second guess it. It was going to be all right. That was the mantra that went around in her head as they left the cabin. He held her hand as they traveled through the woods to the path that would lead up to the inn. The walk took ten minutes, which meant that the cabin was reasonably close to the house. Had his mother heard his howls the night before? The woman probably knew the timbre of each of her sons.

When they stood outside the door, Brina started to tremble slightly. "I'm not sure I can do this, Killian."

He wrapped his arms around her. "You're not alone, Bri. My mother will love you if you give her the chance."

Would she? She hadn't met many mothers, and certainly not in this particular circumstance. Like it or not, though, the two women were stuck with each other. There was nothing that could break the bond between her and Killian. Brina took a deep breath and turned the knob in her hand. Pushing the door open, she walked in front of Killian and braced for impact.

Thankfully, no one was right in the entryway. Part of her hoped that no one was home, but from the smell of bacon in the air, she knew that was unlikely. The sound of heavy boots on the floor caught her attention. Was it one of his brothers? Oh lord, let it not be one of his brothers. They had practically seen Killian ravish her in the forest last night.

"Quite a looker you got there, Killian." Brina turned around to see a much older version of him. She smiled shyly at him and tried to get her voice to work. Thankfully, she didn't have to say a thing.

"Yes, she is. Beautiful, strong, and intelligent," agreed Killian.

She turned to look up at him and found courage in his eyes. When she looked back at Killian's father, she offered her hand. Instead of shaking her hand, the man pulled her into a warm hug.

"Welcome to the family, Brina," he whispered next to her ear.

Brina relaxed against him and let out a soft breath of relief. "Thanks?"

Kenton Knight chuckled when he released her. "That sounds about right. Always carry a fair share of doubt. You never know when my boys will be up to no good. Especially that one."

Killian cleared his throat behind her. "Bri, this is my father, Kenton Knight."

Brina smiled softly. "It's a pleasure to meet you."

"Same. Care for some food? Amber's been cooking up a storm."

Brina almost stumbled over her next words. "I'm not very hungry."

"Nonsense. Come join us." He offered his arm to her, and Brina knew it would be rude to refuse.

Brina took his arm, but looked back at Killian helplessly. She saw his amused smile and wanted to knock it off his face.

Sensing her stress, Kenton patted her hand reassuringly. "I assure you, Amber's bark is worse than her bite."

"Are you sure about that?" she whispered.

Kenton escorted her into a room that was bustling with life, and she wondered how she hadn't heard them before. Three men sat around a table, stuffing their faces as they talked animatedly, about what she didn't know. All conversation stopped the moment Kenton cleared his throat.

"Have you met Brina yet?" He asked them.

Brina offered each of them a half smile. Her eyes looked

around the room, and she was surprised to see that Amber Knight was not in the room. She wasn't sure if this was a reprieve or the forecast of an incoming storm.

"Looking for Mother?" Karter teased her.

Brina almost squeaked her answer. "No."

"She won't bite, much," Karter continued to mess with her.

"Karter!" Killian growled.

"Well, you'd think he'd be in a much better mood after...." Karter's eyes met hers and he had the decency not to finish his words.

Brina held her head high, even though she felt a blush rise on her face. This was what she had signed on for—a lifetime of brothers who were filled with the hijinks of preschoolers. She rolled up her sleeves and took a deep breath. "I'll have you know, his mood has improved greatly." Brina smirked as she reached over and kissed Killian on the cheek. She felt him stiffen slightly, but she didn't take it personally. "But I'm still not above letting him kick your ass if he fancies it."

Kam and Kyle tried to hide their amusement. They both coughed slightly as they tried to stifle their laughs.

"I don't know why you two are laughing. I'm pretty sure he can take both of you at once." She crossed her arms around her and tapped her foot to make her point. "And if he can't, I guarantee I can."

Killian smirked. "Don't mess with a witch when she's angry."

"You should know," taunted Brina. "Anyone else have their two cents to throw in?"

A loud ruckus filled the air as all the men in the room started to laugh loudly. It lasted briefly, before all the air seemed to be sucked out of the room. Brina didn't even have to turn around to know that Amber Knight had walked into the room. Brina held her spine stiff as she turned around to face her.

As if sensing the battle within her, Killian wrapped his arm around her and held her closer. "Mother."

Amber nodded at them. "May I have a word with you, Brina?"

Brina fought the urge to gulp, but she pushed it to the side. She felt his hands pull her closer, but Brina pushed them away. Brina was a grown ass woman. She could handle his mother. "Of course."

Amber led her from the room, and as she did, the room was silent as a morgue. Was Brina walking to the slaughter? Or were they simply hoping to hear the exchange between them? Either way, Brina held her guard up. When they stopped inside what appeared to be a four seasons room, Brina waited to see what would happen next.

"Sit, Brina." Amber gestured to one of the chairs.

Brina was half-tempted to stand on principle. She knew the woman didn't care for her much. Even a blind person could have figured that one out. She sat down across from her and crossed her legs and arms, as if waiting for the inevitable attack.

"I think we got off on the wrong foot," the older woman conceded.

Brina didn't answer her. What could she say? She knew

that Amber had tried to talk her son out of choosing her. Not that she blamed the woman, because honestly, they had only known each other for minutes. But the primal feeling between them was timeless. Brina knew that Killian was the one she had been waiting for. Every bone in her body understood that.

"I've been judgmental."

"Go on...," Brina said softly.

Amber's eyebrows rose curiously. "My, you do have a fair amount of pluck."

"Would you accept any less for Killian?" She challenged her.

"No. They all need a firm hand." A slow smile slid across her face. "You're not afraid of me?"

"Terrified," Brina admitted, but she still refused to back down. "He's worth the risk."

"I'm glad you see that."

"Are you?" Brina only half believed her. "It's pretty clear you don't think I'm good enough for him."

"Goodness...is that what you think?" Amber had the decency to blush guiltily. "I've become his mother after all."

"Excuse me?" Brina uncrossed her arms and looked closer at her.

"Kenton's mother was brutish. A terror in her own right. When he first took me to mate, I thought her eyes would shoot me down on the spot. Of course, she was a werewolf like the men. Not a witch like us. She didn't want them choosing an outsider," Amber explained.

"I can see that." She could. Her mother had always wanted her to find herself a like-minded partner, but Alinda had also believed that the heart took precedence over the mind. Brina knew her mother would have approved of her choice.

"You're generous." Amber sighed. "One day you'll have children of your own to protect. They may all be shifters, maybe not. You'll want them to have the best in life. You may even be so blinded that you forget what it was like to be young and in love."

Love? Her heart skipped a beat. It had been unspoken between them. Their desire for each other had overwritten any need to make the declaration, yet Brina knew that she loved him. Perhaps for her entire life, if she was honest with herself. Although then, he had only been an idea that she had cradled deep inside her.

"I do love him."

"Of course you do, silly girl. Even a fool would recognize that." Amber smiled at her.

Brina returned her smile. "He's pretty remarkable."

"As are you," Amber conceded. "Not every woman could face the challenges of taking a life mate. It's not always easy."

"Nothing ever is." Brina waved her words away.

"No, it isn't." Tears filled the woman's eyes. "I'm sorry if I caused any pain."

Brina reached over and took her hands. "Don't worry. I had a mother once. She was pretty protective too. I think she would have liked you."

"I've never had a daughter before. I've been overpowered in a house filled with testosterone."

"I'm surprised you haven't lost your hair," teased Brina.

"I'd very much like a daughter, if you wouldn't mind."

115

Amber gave her a soft smile.

Brina felt a part of her flutter inside at her words. It would be more than nice to have a mother figure in her life again. She rose from her chair and knelt before her. Brina wrapped her arms around her and gave her a reassuring hug. "I wouldn't mind at all."

A soft shuffle of sound could be heard from the doorway. Two women's voices erupted at once.

"Kenton."

"Killian."

The two men held up their hands and exited the room before another word was uttered. The two women burst out laughing.

"Don't worry, you'll get used to that after a while," assured Amber.

"I don't mind having a built-in radar. I bet it helps keep tabs on them." Brina stood up and offered Amber her hand. "You've been cooking all morning. Maybe it's time to eat."

"Perhaps. Besides, they'll only keep at bay for so long. The Knight pack is more curious than a raccoon chasing a shiny bauble."

Brina giggled at the image. "Should we pretend that we're in an awful row?"

"As much as I love to keep them on their toes, I think we should show our united front." Amber took her hand and followed her out of the room.

When they entered the room, several pairs of eyes were trained on them. Brina shook her head at them. "You really should chew with your mouths closed."

"You'd think I never taught them any manners," Amber clucked her tongue at her sons.

"No time like the present," Brina teased them.

"Oh, I see what you're doing there." Karter spoke first.

"I told you she'd charm her," Kam challenged the rest of them.

"Yeah, but your bet was on Mother. I'm not sure we know who actually won," Karter retorted.

Brina smirked and tapped Karter on the nose. "Guess you'll never know."

When his mouth was left gaping wide open, the rest of the room broke into a chorus of laughter, including Amber Knight, which surprised Brina. She couldn't believe she had been so afraid of her.

Brina walked over to Killian and put her hand in his. He brought it to his mouth and kissed it gently as pride shone in his eyes. She didn't really know what to do with that gesture, for she was still getting used to him. Brina pulled away from him, to his surprise. "What? I'm hungry and there's bacon."

"Bacon?" his father chortled. "Oh, dear. A woman after my own heart."

Brina sat down next to Kenton Knight and let him pile the bacon on her plate. "Oh, that's plenty, thank you."

"Lightweight," he teased her.

"For now." She winked at Killian's father.

"Better get yours while you can, Killian. Apparently, she's worked up quite an appetite," Karter teased him.

"You're just jealous I found her first," Kilian shot back.

Brina reached across the table and touched Karter's hand.

117

"Karter, darling. It would never have worked between us. You're way too immature."

"Boom!" Kyle dropped an imaginary microphone and made an explosion sound.

Karter sighed. "Perhaps. I am better on the eye though."

"You keep telling yourself that," grumbled Killian, who was now sitting down next to her.

Brina retracted her hand and giggled. "You all are too much."

"How's it feel to be surrounded by a loud, obnoxious, rowdy bunch of men?" Kenton asked her.

"I always wondered what it would be like to have a big family. Even overbearing brothers who don't know how to mind their business." Brina turned to Killian. "Is that what you called them, Killian?"

Killian nearly choked on his water. "Bri...."

She slapped him on the back and took one of his arms and started to flap it in the air. "Breathe!"

Kyle shook his head at them. "You really can't make this stuff up."

Brina giggled into her hand prepared for the retribution she saw in Killian's eyes. It was totally worth it. He needed to lighten up just a little. Brina enjoyed the easy back and forth between the family sitting around her. Brina had never realized how much she had missed out on until this moment in time. She hoped they had more than one child. The idea sent a shiver through her, reminding her that this was a conversation they had never had yet.

Brina nibbled on her bottom lip as she pondered all the

things they had yet to discuss. They had already established that she didn't have to stop her work. Where would they live? The cabin was cut off from the rest of the world, and not at all suited to raising children, if he wanted children. She kind of assumed he did, considering he had not taken any precaution against it. Then again, neither had she. Brina had been so lost in the moment that it hadn't even occurred to her. Now that it had, Brina felt slightly conflicted. Not because she didn't want children, but that several steps had already been skipped. Being a mate, was that the same thing as being a wife? Legally?

She pushed her food around her plate for a few seconds before she made her apologies to the table. "Excuse me. I think I need some air."

Chapter 15

Killian watched Brina leave the table. Something was wrong, and he was afraid to find out what. What if she was having second thoughts? In making her his mate, he had changed her life completely. Not only was she stuck with him forever, she was also stuck with everyone in this room. He had not contemplated how that would make her feel.

"What's eating her?" asked Kyle.

"I dunno." Killian looked back to the table around him. Women had always been a mystery to him.

"Did you hurt her?" Kam asked him seriously. Kam looked as if he might like to smash Killian in the face.

"No!" He held his hands up in defense. "Maybe she smelled you?"

Kam sniffed his arm pits. "No, I'm fresh."

"Give her some space," suggested his mother.

"Your mother's right. A lot has happened to her in a very short period of time." Kenton agreed with his wife.

Karter whistled loudly. "You done messed something up. I smell turbulence ahead."

"Shut it." Killian was really close to knocking that grin off his brother's face. It had been a week since the last time he'd smashed it, although they had been shifted at the time. They often took their frustrations out on each other. But now that Killian had mated, maybe the aggression from the rest of the pack would subside. It came with the territory, unfortunately.

"Did you find out what she came here for?" Kenton asked.

"Investigating Witch's Hollow," Killian answered.

He had wondered what had really brought her here. Fate, perhaps? Not that Killian had ever put stock in destiny or the notion that things happened for a reason. To him, everything was a choice. Brina could just as easily have made the choice to set him aside. He wouldn't have blamed her in the least. Although, he would have yearned for her the rest of his life, even if he had claimed someone else. His wolf would never have let him forget her. She'd called to both of them, starting with the minute she touched him outside Witch's Hollow, to protect him. Even now, the idea of her trying to keep him safe made him feel like chuckling. At the time, she had no idea that he was the one thing that could be the most dangerous for her. He had tried to protect her from that, but neither one of them seemed able to deny the desire that swirled between them.

"Why?" asked Kam.

Killian blinked. He looked at his brother and smirked. "What?"

"Earth to Killian. Why did she come to investigate Witch's

ELISSA DAYE

Hollow?" Even Kyle seemed to find the situation amusing.

"She's a witch too, Kam," Amber tried to explain to her sons.

"Like that explains anything." Karter rolled his eyes.

"Um...I don't think I actually got around to asking her that." The reason for her arrival hadn't mattered to him the minute his wolf had attached itself to her scent. He had clearly been distracted. Even now he was thinking about sinking inside her sweet core. Killian felt himself stiffen, and he adjusted in his seat slightly.

Karter snorted. "Thinking with your—"

"Karter!" Amber interrupted him. "Manners."

"What? I was going to say wolf." Clearly, Karter was going to say nothing of the sort.

"Like hell," Kyle chuckled.

"Boys." Their mother threw her hands up in the air. It was probably the third time she had done so that day.

"So, what happened yesterday?" Kenton interrupted.

"Well, Killian got la—"

"Karter, so help me, if you finish that...." Killian slammed his fist on the table. Heaven help the woman who fell for that idiot.

"Boys, if you're going to tear into each other, would you do it away from the fine china?" Amber Knight sighed in defeat.

"I heard the four of you outside in the afternoon. Was there a problem?" Kenton redirected the conversation.

"Well, she heard the Calling."

Killian did not want to answer that question. There had

been many witches who had heard what they all knew as the Calling. It was some magnetic pull that came over them when they reached the glen near Witch's Hollow. Many witches had been lost to it over the years. That was one of the reasons the pack kept a close eye on the river. Killian didn't like to think what would have happened if he hadn't made it to her in time. She had been so close to the hole that sucked people into its hidden depths — not to mention the lack of control over her faculties would have made it far easier to drown in the current.

"What was she doing near the glen? Didn't you tell her about it?" Amber asked her son.

"Apparently he's not much of a talker," teased Kam.

"Talking's overrated," Karter added to the fray.

"Talkers are overcompensating," agreed Kyle.

Killian rubbed his temples. He was growing increasingly frustrated with the conversation around him. Not to mention the fact that if they continued to insinuate anything dirty, he would not be able to control the erection that threatened to make itself quite visible. He hadn't been this randy since he was a teenager.

"Boys, this is no laughing matter." Kenton's voice rose slightly. "We need to find out who's causing this."

"Agreed." Amber backed her husband, who looked at her like she was sick.

"You feeling all right there?" He asked her.

"Why?" She asked him cautiously.

"You never let me be right." He grinned at her.

Killian watched the easy banter between his parents.

One day he would have that with Brina. Their relationship was in the raw, formative phase, but he knew they would get through it. He was not disappointed in his choice for his mate, not one bit. Every minute he learned something new about her that made his feelings grow for her. Seeing the way she dealt with his brothers, accepted his mother, those were things that made him incredibly proud to call her his. He wanted to shout it from the rooftops, but for now he would settle for just one more kiss from her delicate lips. Perhaps a taste of her...well, anything. Killian's gut clenched.

Killian had warned her that she could have no one else. He prayed she understood that, because he wasn't sure who would be more infuriated, the man or the beast. Heaven help the man who tried to come between them. There would be hell to pay. He felt his hair rising on the back of his neck, and his eyes flashed just thinking about it.

"Maybe it's time to go to the witch's camp," suggested Karter.

Killian rolled his eyes. "Which one are you planning on visiting?"

"Any number of them now that I'm a free agent."

Killian shook his head at his brother. Now that Killian had found his mate, the rest of them were off the hook for a small window of time. They could go back on the prowl now that their alpha had chosen. Killian still couldn't believe his father had given up leadership so easily. He was still quite young, but sometimes there was no rhyme or reason to it.

Kam grumbled, "Easy for you to say."

"Still off limits?" Killian asked him. So, maybe not all

of them. It was different for each of them. Their beast fully controlled their desires, more than any of them cared to admit. Man and beast were so in tune that what one did affected the other. Sometimes, irreparably.

"We're working on it," Kam answered gruffly.

"That must mean you're next," his mother suggested as Kam bristled slightly.

"Just imagine the old ball and chain waiting for you. Maybe you can find someone closer to your age to put up with your ass," suggested Karter.

"Want me to punch him?" offered Killian.

"Nah. I'll get him when he least expects it, like I always do." Kam ground his fist into his hand.

"Says you," Karter snickered.

"Karter, you realize you get twice as many poundings as the rest of them, right?" Amber Knight cautioned him.

"Whatever. I give quite a few too."

"In an alternate dimension, maybe," Kyle snorted next to him. "The only one who's gotten more is Kendrick."

"Speaking of Kendrick, when is his next break?" Karter asked.

"Thanksgiving," Kenton answered them. Any time someone brought up Kendrick, his chest seemed to puff up in pride. Kendrick was twenty-four, and pursuing his anthropology masters.

Killian tired of the conversation. His growing need for his mate couldn't be put off any longer. Not to mention the fact that he was really starting to worry about Brina. When they mated, their souls had intertwined. He sensed the melancholy that was drifting inside her. It was time to put her at ease, for whatever was causing her to be upset.

He shoved his plate away from him. "I think I'm done with my food too."

As Killian pushed away from the table, he saw his mother's smile.

"Good luck," she offered him.

Killian had the feeling he was going to need it. Women were unpredictable creatures—maybe not as volatile as a werewolf's beast, but still unnerving. The only woman Killian had ever had to understand was his mother. Somehow Killian had the feeling that Brina was very much like his mother. Soft, determined, vulnerable, powerful, insecure, independent. She was a puzzle of which he would spend the rest of his life unlocking the pieces one at a time. He looked forward to it, but even more, he looked forward to the moments they would have now.

Killian closed his eyes and remembered the eyelids that had fluttered slow with desire, and his gut clenched. Yes, it was time to find his mate.

Chapter 16

Brina sat in the garden on a bench she was pretty sure was one of Amber Knight's favorite places. Very few flowers were blooming, but there was a handful of different herbs that Brina recognized—some for healing, some for cooking. She saw the lavender bushes and smiled. Amber must put a sprig of lavender in with the linens to keep them smelling so fresh. All things Brina had picked up over the years.

She sighed and a slow tear worked its way down her face. Had Amber known all she was giving up to raise this pack of men? Or was it tossed at her so quickly she couldn't second guess it? Not that Brina would have made a different choice later, she just was unsure where she fit right now.

Between his sheets? Brina knew she would always fit there, happily too. But what about the other areas of their lives? What did he do? Did he have a profession? Brina realized she had never asked him. In other relationships they would have spent many hours, days, even months getting to

127

know each other. The only thing she really knew was the way she felt about him.

And if she felt this way, chances were so did Killian. Desiring her was one thing—loving her was something different altogether, and while their bodies simulated those feelings, there was no actual proof that it existed between either one of them. What a tangled web she had thrown herself carelessly into. What if she wasn't enough? Then Killian had united with someone who would eventually destroy him.

"Bri?" His voice was soft and filled with concern.

She quickly wiped away her tears and offered him a weak smile. "Killian."

Killian sat down next to her. He looked into her eyes as he wiped away her tears. "Are you okay?"

Brina didn't know how to answer. She started with the truth. "I'm confused."

Killian looked away from her and cursed softly. "You have regrets?"

"No...not really." She touched his face so he turned around to look at her. "No regrets, Killian. But I'm worried you might."

He smiled at her. "Never."

"Killian...."

"Yes, Bri?"

"We don't even know each other." She threw it out there and let it marinade before them.

"I know enough."

"I don't," she argued.

"What do you need to know?" He asked her.

"What happens next?" Brina's mouth wobbled slightly. "You see, for the rest of us there's marriage, children...."

"I see." His eyes twinkled merrily. "Is that what this is about?"

"I don't know how I fit. What is this? I'm your mate, but what does that mean?" Very few things terrified Brina, but waiting for his answer made her on edge. She hadn't even figured out what she wanted in life. At one point she'd thought marriage and kids, but that had seemed to slip away over the years as something completely unobtainable. Right now, she was now committed to him for the rest of her life, but they had not defined what that commitment was.

"I have done this backwards. I'm sorry for that. I'm not usually this impulsive." His eyes were filled with regret. "What do you want, Bri?"

Brina blinked in confusion. What did she want? "To *know you*."

"I see."

Killian pulled her into his lap, and his lips came down to hers. Brina felt her breath stop in her chest when she felt the bulge near her thigh. How could he already be...? Her thoughts were cut off completely when his tongue slipped into her mouth. She sighed against him. Here, like this, doubt seemed to slip away with ease. They would always have this. But what happened in the other moments, when they had to figure out where their lives were going?

Killian broke the kiss and his eyes flashed before her. "You do know me, Bri."

"Not *all* of you."

129

Killian's eyebrows rose as he remembered their moments together. "I'd say you know me pretty well."

"Killian!" Brina slapped him on the arm. "I know your body, but not your mind, or your heart for that matter."

"Bri...I thought you knew." He lifted her hand to his mouth and kissed it gently. "I belong to you, mind, body, heart, and soul."

Brina did not react to his declaration. It was just a flourish, a deflection. "Do you love me?"

"Yes, Bri. I love you." His face took on a serious light.

"Why?" She crossed her arms in front of her and demanded a proper answer.

"For just that reason." He pointed to her posture, "You're obstinate, pushy, fierce, devoted, unafraid, determined, soft, sweet, tender, forgiving, relentless, intelligent, beautiful, and kind."

"How do you know all that?" Brina had trouble believing his words.

"Bri, I don't need a lifetime to know my heart. I've waited a long time for the right woman. I wouldn't settle for anything less." He kissed her forehead. "Fortunately, I've got all those things, and so much more, in my arms."

Another tear formed in her eye. She had never heard anyone say such beautiful things to her before. Some of her doubts started to slip away. "So, it's not just about sex?"

Killian stiffened beneath her. "Bri...."

"What?" She waited for him to defend against her accusation.

"Don't say that right now...I'm having enough trouble

keeping myself in line," Killian cautioned her.

"Sex?" She asked him in confusion.

Killian growled and his mouth came down on hers as the desire that had been building in him made itself known. Brina felt a slow wave of desire work its way into her bones as she wrapped her arms around his neck and pulled him closer.

Killian pulled his mouth away from hers and his breathing was shallow. "I want you more than the air I breathe, Bri."

"Is that enough, Killian? One day, it might not be." Her lips wobbled slightly.

Killian ran a hand through his hair and let out a frustrated breath. "That's it."

He stood up, and she almost fell off his lap. He grabbed her hand and started to pull her along with him. Brina tugged against his hand slightly. "Where are we going?"

"To *talk*." He grinned at her, and Brina had the distinct feeling that he wanted to do a whole lot more than just talk. If he turned on his charm, there was nothing she could do to fight it. Her body craved his touch even now. She shivered slightly as anticipation filled her.

Brina lost count of time as they walked quietly through the forest to the cabin where he had made her his one true mate. When they were standing outside it, she wanted to refuse to enter. It was hard enough to string two thoughts together when she was around him, but the minute they entered there, she knew it would all be over.

"You're not afraid, are you?" Killian sensed her hesitation.

"A little." She was honest. "But not of you."

"Good." He opened the door and gestured for her to

enter.

Brina felt desire oozing off him when she walked past him, and it made her heart skip a beat. When he closed the door behind them, she turned to face him. His face was conflicted, and she understood it. She stepped toward him, and attempted to touch his face.

Killian stepped back from her hand. "If you touch me, there'll be no talking. Now, sit."

Brina pouted softly, feeling very much like a child who got caught with her hand in the cookie jar. She walked over to the couch near the fire and curled her legs up under her. Killian sat in the chair across from her. Even though he was so close to her, the distance made him feel so far away. She patted the couch next to her. "I won't bite, Killian."

"Pity," he murmured. "I think I'll stay right here."

Brina sighed. "What you said—"

"I love you, Bri. I intend to spend my life proving it." His voice was soft and serious.

She smiled at him. An idea popped into her head, one that could take care of two birds with one stone. Brina got up from the couch and stood before him.

"What are you doing, Bri?"

"For everything you share, I'll take off one piece of clothing."

Hot molten lava—his eyes were now full of it. "I don't think that's a good idea."

"I won't touch you," Brina promised—half-heartedly though, because it wasn't one she intended to keep forever. "And for everything I share, you will take something off."

"And when we run out of clothes?" His eyebrow rose curiously.

"Then you get to make one wish at a time."

"A wish? Like...?"

"Let's say, I want you to kiss me, then you have to do that." Brina knelt before him and looked into his eyes. "You're not afraid of me, are you?"

"*Never.*" His breath caught in his throat when Brina moved closer to him.

"Tell me something I don't know about you."

"I'm the leader of my pack, but I'm not the oldest. I'm thirty-two." Kilian waited to see what she would take off.

Brina reached down and took off a shoe. "You look disappointed."

He chuckled. "Maybe. We'll get to that. What is your favorite color?"

"Green, but that was a fluff question. Ask me something harder," she challenged him.

"How many men have you slept with?" Jealousy flashed in his eyes.

Brina put a finger to her head and started to add up the relationships where she'd actually had sex. "Counting you?"

"Yes."

"Does the wolf count too?" Brina asked him.

"No...." He was losing patience with her.

"Four. I lost my virginity to a very untalented teenage boy, who barely broke my maidenhead. The second was a man I dated for a few months in college. The third was someone I trusted, but as soon as.... Well, let's just say I was a horrible disappointment to him. And then...well, there was you."

"Idiots, all of them." He let out a frustrated breath. "Just the idea of them putting their hands on you...."

Brina smiled at him. "I answered your question. What are you going to lose?"

Killian almost ripped his shirt off. "Ask away." Brina stared at his muscled flesh and closed her eyes as she tried to capture it in her mind. She must have taken too long, because Killian's voice interrupted her. "Bri?"

"Oh, right." She licked her lips and tried to remember that there was a point to all of this.

"Bri...." His voice was almost a growl.

"How many women have you slept with?"

"Too many to count, but the only one that matters to me is you." His face was shuttered, as if he was waiting for her to get upset with his answer.

She smiled at him. "I'm not surprised, really."

"Oh? Why's that?"

"Any woman who didn't want to jump your bones would have to be blind. I'm going to have to carry a broomstick."

"Why?" He asked her cautiously.

"To beat them off you." She pulled her other shoe off.

Killian chuckled. "You have nothing to worry about."

"Oh, I know. Your turn."

"How do you like your eggs?"

"Scrambled with cheese, why?" she asked him.

"Because by the time I'm done with you, you're going to be starving." Killian removed one of his shoes.

Brina sure hoped so. "What do you do, besides watch

over the forest? Do you have a job?"

"I like to work with my hands. I'm a carpenter and I make furniture."

"Did you make the rocking chair?" She asked him.

"Yes, and that's two questions. Strip it down, Bri," he ordered her.

Brina smiled. "As you wish."

She moved back to the couch and removed her shirt, followed by her bra. When she saw the raw hunger on his face, Brina felt a tremor work its way through her body. She didn't bother to hide herself. Instead, she sat there with her chest displayed proudly. "Your turn."

Killian blinked, then shook his head slightly. "Do you want children?"

Brina hadn't expected that question. She looked away from him, and paused as she tried to figure out what it was that she did want. Closing her eyes, she imagined a smaller version of him crawling over the floor, and her heart warmed over. "Yes. If we're lucky, a few. I would hate for them to be lonely."

Her answer seemed to make him happy. He took off his other shoe. "Good. When can we get started?"

Brina sighed. "The game's not over yet, Killian. Cat or dog?"

"Both. But that was too easy. Pick another one," he challenged her.

"What are you afraid of most in life?" She asked him.

He didn't skip a beat. "Losing you."

Her breath caught in her throat. Brina couldn't look at

him. She stood up and removed her pants. When she sat down, she didn't see desire in his eyes, just an overwhelming love that caught her by surprise. "Your turn, Killian."

"Will you marry me?"

Brina sucked in her breath and a tear slid down her face. "Yes."

Killian rose from his chair and knelt before her. He put his hands on her face and whispered, "Just one kiss, Brina."

When his lips touched hers, Brina felt all her doubts start to fade away. Gentle, sweet, filled with the promise of something that was eternal. When she tried to deepen the kiss, her breasts scarred his flesh and he pulled away.

"Brina," he cautioned her as he removed one of his socks.

She pouted when he pulled away. "Fine. Is this your house?"

"Yes, one of them."

One? How many houses did he have? She was suddenly filled with even more questions, but she might lose her mind before she got to them. Removing her panties, she flung them at his feet.

He was clearly having trouble staying focused. He cleared his throat. "Do you mind settling down near my family?"

She smiled at them. "Not as long as the windows have blinds and the doors have locks."

Killian looked relieved as he removed his other sock, but he didn't say a word. His eyes traced every inch of her body with almost as much heat as his hands would have.

Brina gulped slightly as the thought of her having her wicked way with him rose to the front of her mind, game be damned. But she also didn't want to forfeit. She would just have to try that much harder to get him to break the rules. With only two socks left, Brina was fairly certain that the exciting part was just about to get started.

"Does it hurt?" she asked him.

"What?"

"Shifting. It looks rather painful." She gave him a weak smile.

"Sometimes, but it all comes with the territory. The Knights have been protecting this world for as long as I can remember."

Brina removed a sock. "Me too. Protecting, that is. That's why I came here. I was called to help."

"How long have you been practicing?" He asked her.

"All my life. I'm a hereditary. Our magic has been passed down to the women every generation."

Killian removed his belt and Brina smirked at him. "What? A belt is technically an article of clothing."

Brina grumbled. "I should have worn my earrings."

He chuckled at her. "Not my fault, Bri."

"Would you be upset if you knew I was rich?"

"How rich?" His eyebrow rose curiously.

"Disgustingly so." Brina had never really lived her live as the millionaire that she was. It was much easier to live a simpler life. "And you didn't answer my question."

"No. That means you're not after my money," he teased her.

Brina removed her last sock and stretched out on the couch in all her naked glory. Her hand moved over her stomach, and she waited to see what Killian would do next.

"Dominant or submissive?" he threw out at her.

"I'm not sure. Can we try both sometime?" she asked him.

Killian almost bolted off the chair. He stood up and to remove his jeans but didn't. "God, I hope so. The idea of you taming the beast...."

Brina shuddered at the thought. Would she be able to wield the control over Killian and his beast? "Has it merits, doesn't it?"

"Well, Brina, do you have another question?" His eyes gleamed.

"I'm at a loss," she pouted.

"Then you forfeit this round. Let's see...what do I want?" He thought for a moment. "Touch yourself."

"Excuse me?" she squeaked. Touch herself? With him watching? "Where?"

"All over."

Brina pursed her lips. He wasn't seriously suggesting she do that. She narrowed her eyes on him.

"Your rules, Brina," he reminded her.

Damn it. He was right. Those were the rules. She took a deep breath and closed her eyes. She started to move her hand and he interrupted her.

"Eyes open, Bri."

Her eyes flew open and she saw the hunger on his face. "I'm not sure I can do this."

"Remember, unafraid."

Brina kept her eyes on his face, watching his expression as she moved her hands down to her breasts. She moved

138

them gently around each areola, which already seemed to harden. Squeezing her nipples in her fingers, she sucked in her breath when she saw the madness cross over his face. She released them and let her hands slide down her stomach, and let herself imagine it was his hands touching her. Her belly clenched in reflex. When her hands started to travel lower, Killian growled. "That's enough."

"You sure?" she whispered.

"No...yes." He ran a hand through his hair as he tried to clear his thoughts.

"Your question," she reminded him.

"Did you like that?" his voice was almost ragged.

Had she? Probably more than she cared to admit. It wasn't something she would normally do. "Yes...."

Killian sucked in his breath at her answer. He undid his jeans and slid them down slowly. "I'm running out of clothes."

"Good." Brina could see his erection bulging tightly against his briefs. She licked her lips as she thought about what she could do with it.

"Stop that." His voice sounded like he was almost in pain.

"What?" She bit her lip, perplexed by his command.

"Is that your question?" He asked her.

"Yes."

"You're playing with fire. This will be over before it's begun. I'm trying to be a good boy," he teased her.

"Oh, you're good. You're very good." Brina closed her eyes and remembered the passion that had flowed so easily between the two of them, and she almost sighed aloud.

"Kiss me, Bri."

139

She was happy to oblige him. Brina slid to the floor and crawled over to him. Her mouth rose to his and he kissed her gently on the mouth. He was maintaining his control far better than she was. When he broke the kiss, Brina moved away from him and sat on the floor with her legs wide open.

"Bri!" He almost shouted at her.

"What?" she asked innocently.

"Close your legs." The veins on his neck were nearly exposed. Brina could sense his wolf creeping closer to her, as it fought for control over his passion.

"What's your favorite position?" he asked her.

"Hmm...I'm not sure. But I'm willing to experiment." She smiled brightly at him. "I rather enjoyed when you took me from behind."

Brina had never seen a man take his bottoms off in her lifetime, but as he did his cock sprung into the open air and Brina felt a fierce need circle inside her. She barely heard him call her name.

"Bri...Bri?"

She looked up to his grinning face. He was enjoying the effect he had over her. "Yes?"

"It's your question," he reminded her.

"Hmm...how many orgasms can you have each day?"

Her question caught him completely off guard. His teeth clenched and his cock seemed to bounce in reflex. "Depends on the day. Sometimes three, sometimes six. Come here, Bri," he ordered her.

"What was your wish?" She asked him.

"You'll see."

"I don't know about that; you seem a little enraged," she teased him.

"Bri...." His voice was almost guttural.

Bri stood up before him. "Yes, Killian?"

He pulled her onto his lap and his mouth was on her. Readjusting her in his lap, he slid her over his length and Brina almost came undone. His hips moved slowly at first, heating his path into her. Brina whimpered when his hands squeezed her ass. He helped guide her up and down, until Brina finally understood she could take whatever she wanted from him.

"That's it, Bri. Take it," he whispered against her ear.

She rode his length, taking him slow, then fast, until she felt the tiny explosion erupting inside her. Killian tensed against her and held himself still while she finished her orgasm. When she opened her eyes, she looked into his. She was desperate for more. "Please, Killian." He pulled her down hard on his length and she almost screamed. "Yes, please...."

That was all he needed to hear. He rammed into her over and over, taking every inch of her as the beast inside fused with him. Brina sense the need in him, and she met each thrust with her own. Her release was building inside, but it refused to let go until she felt him jerking wildly under her. They came together as one, and Brina collapsed on top of him.

Killian held her tightly against him and stroked her back as he pulsated inside her. "I may have undercalculated that number."

Brina smiled at him. "We could always test that number out."

141

"Later, Bri. I have to get to work."

She pouted at him. "Just as well. So do I."

"Don't go into the forest without someone with you," he cautioned her.

"Who should I take with me? Karter?" She suggested.

"Like hell. Take Kam if he's free. Or my father. Yes, take him with you."

"Don't trust me?" she sighed.

"Oh, it's not you I don't trust."

"They're harmless, Killian. I only have eyes for you." She rubbed her nose against his.

"Ah, Bri. Until tonight?"

"Is that a promise?" She squeezed herself around his erection, which was still hard enough to imagine doing so much more to.

"Guarantee."

Brina pulled herself off him and reached down to retrieve her clothes. When she looked back at him, he had a serious look on his face. "Something wrong?"

He smiled slowly. "Just imagining what you'll look like when you're thick with child."

Brina blushed. For all she knew that thought had already taken root. She smiled. "Someday."

She quickly left the room before she got in trouble for distracting him further. When she made it up to the master, she heard the door open downstairs. It closed again, and she realized he had already left. Brina lay down on his side of the bed and breathed in his scent. She wished she could bottle the scent and carry it with her always.

Chapter 17

As Brina lay on the bed, she wondered what could be so important that Killian had to rush off for it. He had said he was a carpenter. Did that mean he had a job to do? The man would probably always be a mystery to her.

Brina sighed. Well, she could sit here and wait to see what would happen next, or she could go out and start to live her life a little. He had asked her not to go into the woods without him, to bring someone else with her. The only problem with that was she wasn't entirely sure how to get back to the main house from here. Was there a path?

After checking herself over in the mirror, Brina walked downstairs. She was actually surprised to find Kam sitting on the couch waiting for her. "Kam."

"Hello, Brina. Killian thought I could be of service."

"Of course he did." Apparently, the man thought of everything.

"How can I help?" Kam asked her.

"Well, first, I'd like to know how I find my way back to the inn."

"Sure thing." He rose from the couch, and she wondered just how long he had been sitting there.

"You got here awfully quick. How did you know?" Brina asked him.

"I wasn't far away." Kam opened the door and waved his arm before him. "After you, my lady."

She sure hoped he hadn't been anywhere outside the cabin. Had he heard them? God, she hoped not. Brina shoved that thought to the back of her mind. She couldn't let the distractions get in the way today. Brina really wanted to get some investigating done.

Kam pointed to the posts that had been driven into the ground. "If you follow those markers, they will lead you back."

"I see. I'm not sure how I missed those before." Brina felt like she was losing her touch.

"You were probably just distracted. Happens to the best of us."

"Well, your brother is certainly a distraction. One I hadn't counted on."

"Are you happy, Brina?" Kam asked her quietly.

"Not to worry, Kam. I am happy."

Kam looked relieved. "Good. I'd hate to have to hurt him."

"He's a good man, Kam. Although, I'm only really getting started with him. I imagine we'll both have our days when we clash. All couples do, right?"

"I wouldn't know. I haven't been in a real relationship." Kam held his hands up in front of him when he saw the assumption in her eyes. "Oh, I've plenty of experience with women."

Brina chuckled. "Oh, the look on your face, Kam."

"That's just not funny." His nose twitched in annoyance.

"I've never had a brother before. Am I not allowed to tease you?" She didn't want to upset him, especially if Killian trusted him the most.

Kam blinked and started laughing. "Oh! You're too innocent, Yes, anything goes in the Knight household, although I wouldn't bring up sexual relationships in front of Killian. He'd likely kill us for even talking about it."

"He does seem the jealous type." Not that it bothered her. She had never had a man who cared that much about her. Most men were more likely to push her to the side rather than fight for her.

"Might be the alpha in him," suggested Kam.

Brina decided to switch the topic. "So, the small posts lead back to the house. How might I find Witch's Hollow?"

Kam's face now seemed paler. "What do you want with Witch's Hollow?"

"I was sent here to investigate the murders that have been happening the last few years."

"How do you know about them?" He looked uneasy.

"You do realize I'm a witch, right?" Brina's eyes narrowed on him.

"Well, yes, but no one on the outside knows what is really happening here. The law enforcement thinks it's just

145

accidental drownings." Kam stood there, slightly perplexed.

"Someone from the inside sent for me." Brina waited for his next question.

"Who?"

"The dead." Brina sighed and prepared for his reaction to her statement.

"Really? A two-for?"

"Excuse me?" What the hell did he mean by that?

"You know...a witch and a psychic medium. Two for one, like the rest of us." He grinned at her.

Brina almost sighed in relief. "I guess you could think of it that way."

"So, the witches are speaking to you from the grave? What did they tell you?"

"They aren't sure what's causing it. They believe it's an outside force. I'd really like to check out Witch's Hollow to see if I can get any impressions from it. Can you take me there?" Brina sure hoped Kam had more of an adventurous spirit, and that he didn't *always* answer to his brother.

"I won't tell, if you won't." Kam winked at her.

"That's the spirit. Now, how do we find it?" If she was going to live anywhere near here, Brina would need to know where she was at all times. She certainly didn't expect to spend more time than necessary in the hollow, though.

"The trick is finding the path that leads there." He nodded for her to follow him. "It's quite a walk."

"That's okay. I'm wearing my walking shoes, and I'm not afraid of a little exercise." Brina found that she was actually wide awake. Maybe it was all the extra exercise, not that she would tell Kam that. That's all she needed. The brothers would never let Killian live it down, and in the end, it would only humiliate her.

"This way." Kam led her through the first line of trees.

At least these trees looked familiar. She had walked through here last night when she had found Killian. In fact, there was the rock she'd sat on right in the middle of the small clearing. She was pretty sure she could find this area. From here, though, she had no idea.

"Do you see that oak with the large bend at the top?"

Brina looked at the tree he was pointing to. It had one large fork that almost seemed to be pointing to the east. "That's a massive tree."

"It's been struck by lightning eight times, and it still stands tall."

"Wow. That's almost divine intervention," Brina remarked.

"It's intervention for sure. That tree marks the path leading down to Witch's Hollow. The tree is protected by an ancient magic."

"I see." And she did. Brina started to walk toward it, leaving Kam standing there staring at her in shock.

"Where are you going?"

"To Witch's Hollow." She rolled her eyes at him, as if he was a marble short. Brina was pretty sure she had already made herself pretty clear.

"Not alone, you're not."

"Then what are you waiting for?" She teased him.

Kam looked as if he would rather be anywhere right now

but here. "You can't just march into it. It's—"

"I'm a witch, Kam. I know how to protect myself...at least when I'm not distracted." She had a feeling he would bring up the river, so she put that out there. "I promise not to let any voices lead me astray this time. Besides, I have you. Unless you're too afraid."

"I'm not afraid." Kam's chest puffed up in defense.

"Then what's the problem?"

"Our kind are not allowed...not inside the ring," Kam tried to explain.

"Hmm...so you can't go inside, yet you can't leave me alone. Sucks to be you." She fought the urge to roll her eyes at him as she kept moving. Brina wasn't about to let him talk her out of it.

"Fine. I'll go with you and keep an eye on you from the tree line." He cursed softly. "Killian's going to kill me."

"Don't worry. I'll deal with him." She smiled at Kam, who had the decency to blush at her words. "Let's go. Daylight's wasting away here."

Brina walked beside Kam in silence. She was pretty sure Kam was trying to find fifty different ways to talk her out of going into the hollow. None of them would work—maybe he knew that too. As the trees twisted around her, she saw that the bark seemed to be darker the closer they got to the clearing ahead. When Kam stopped next to her, Brina turned to smile at him. "Don't worry. I'll be careful."

"If something happens—"

"You'll come racing to help me." Brina knew Kam wouldn't leave her out there to get harmed, no matter what happened inside the circle. The Knight men would always protect one of their own. "I won't be long, Kam."

He nodded to her and looked over to the left, where there was another large rock. "I'll be there."

"Thank you, Kam."

"For what?" He looked surprised.

"Understanding." She smiled at him.

"My mother's a witch too. Pigheaded to boot. I know better than to stir that pot." He winked at her.

"Good man. Maybe you should teach your brother that," she teased him.

"Hell no! It's more fun to watch him dig his own hole." He chortled in laughter.

Brina rolled her eyes and shook her head. Men! She continued toward the hollow, but before she stepped inside it, she felt its energy flowing around her. Brina closed her eyes and quickly conjured a shield to protect herself from it. She did not want a repeat of the day before. If she had shielded herself then, the voice would not have been able to manipulate her. Lessons were often difficult to swallow, but life was certainly filled with them.

Taking a deep breath, Brina was ready to enter Witch's Hollow. As she walked, she could see an aura of lights swarming around her, as testament to the current of magic that wove its tentacles around any intruders. It was this very magic that kept the Knight pack from entering. Too bad it couldn't keep out the dark casters as well. But then again, balance was always key. If one power had too much control everything else in this area could be thrown off kilter.

In the middle of the clearing were five large stones that were placed to represent the different elements. She could see white lines of energy flowing between them, creating a pentacle of energy the witches in the area used as their gathering circle. As she walked closer to it, she could also see the burnt lines in the grass, where some entity had made an inverse symbol to counteract the energy inside. She didn't think the dark casters would have desecrated the area like this. While they were working with different energy, there was often a mutual respect still.

The closer she got to it, the stronger was the wave of energy surrounding her. Brina started to wonder if her shield would be enough. The hair rose on the back of her neck, and she heard the familiar whisper calling to her again.

Come.

"Not this time." She crossed her arms over her chest and held her ground.

Witch! His voice accused her.

Brina felt a shiver up her spine. She reached down to touch the grass and closed her eyes. As she did, an image of an older man popped into her head, then disappeared. Definitely a male. Someone who was channeling something evil to kill the witches around here.

Opening her eyes, she went to the large flat boulder in the middle of the circle. This was where the witches created their altar for when they gave thanks to the goddess above. She could see dried wax at different places around it, but something else was there too. Was that blood?

Brina leaned over to look closer. Definitely a liquid, not a solid, but she wasn't about to touch it. If this man was using this space, he could easily have sacrificed a living thing in one of his rituals. It would have to be cleansed properly, and she didn't have the tools on her to do so. Perhaps the witches at the camp would know more about it.

Brina took a deep breath and closed her eyes again. She let her energy pour through her, connecting all the points in her body until she was able to activate her third eye, her spiritual lens that would allow her to see the other plane around her. When she was ready, she opened her eyes and saw a large grid of light around her. These lines were ley lines. If she followed them, she might be able to find from where this being was drawing its energy.

"Brina," cautioned Kam from the line of trees.

"I'm fine, Kam. You worry too much." He was right though. Someone or something was getting extremely upset with her presence. It did not want to be found. That was too bad. He would have to be brought down sooner rather than later.

"*Brina.*" Killian's voice was right behind her.

She turned on her heels and squeaked. "Killian! Goodness, you scared me."

"Good, you should be scared."

Brina narrowed an eye on him. "What are you doing here? I thought you were working."

"I was...until Kam texted me."

Brina turned an accusatory glare on Kam. "Spoil sport!"

"Bri!" Killian almost growled at her.

"You're not supposed to be in here," Brina reminded him.

She saw the hair standing up on his arms. She took pity on him and extended her shield to surround him. "Better?"

"No," he grumbled. "We're done here."

Brina let out an exasperated sigh. "Fine, but I haven't seen where the ley lines lead to."

"Nowhere good." Killian was dead serious.

Brina saw the terror in his eyes. Was he afraid of what lurked there? Or afraid of what could have happened to her? She found the fear more disturbing than the anger. Killian didn't strike her as someone who was afraid of anything. "Well, if you won't let me investigate it, will you at least take me to the witch camp?"

"Tomorrow."

"Fine." She gave him a half-smile. "You did tell me I could go into the forest."

"I didn't know you were going to come here," he argued.

"You know why I'm here. I'm not going to stop my investigation. Are you planning on watching me twenty-four seven?"

"I've got plenty of people to help me." His teeth were gritted.

Brina felt like hitting him. He was not the boss of her. Why did men always think they could make all the decisions? Her bottom lip trembled in anger, but she didn't say a word. Turning around, she left the clearing the way she had entered. When Kam tried to offer her an apologetic smile, she glared at him.

Both of them tried to engage her in conversation as they walked back to the cabin, but Brina refused to talk to either of them. The two of them stayed at the outskirts just outside the cabin, talking about her more than likely. Brina was so angry she went inside the cabin and retrieved her keys and purse. She was about to leave, but then remembered her car was having issues. She decided to take her chances. Brina needed to get out of here before she said something that would really get her into trouble.

Chapter 18

Brina stomped through the forest, every inch of her seething with rage. She knew he was the alpha of his pack, but damned if she would let him dictate every inch of her life. Just when she thought things would be okay between them, he had to go and be a complete asshat. He'd better watch himself. She'd mount his hide on the mantle if he didn't back off.

Mount him? She giggled. Suddenly, a totally different image popped into her head. "Get a grip, Brina."

That's right. Hang on to the anger. He had to learn that it wasn't okay to boss her around. She followed the markers leading back to the inn. When she made her way to her car, she opened the door and tried to start it up. Again, nothing. "Damn it."

"Would you like me to fix it?" A voice startled her.

"Oh, Mr. Knight. You scared me." She put a hand to her heart as she took a deep breath.

"You seem upset. And call me Kenton." He opened the door for her and offered his hand.

"Thank you. Yes. I'm furious." Her nose twitched and she started to shake visibly. "Your son is an egotistical buffoon!"

"I can see that. Care to come in for some tea?" He asked her with merry eyes.

"I've a mind to skin him, one inch at a time." She sighed. "Yes, tea would be lovely, thank you."

"Amber's a good ear," suggested Kenton.

A tear gathered in her eye as she realized she didn't really have anyone to talk to. She had never felt so lonely in her life. Surrounded by people for the first time, she realized how much of an outsider she was to everything. She let him lead her inside to the kitchen, where Killian's mother was already making tea.

"How did you know?"

"I've been there. Kenton, why don't you take the boys out somewhere?" suggested Amber.

"Even—"

"Especially Killian," she ordered him.

Brina watched Kenton leave the room and looked at her in awe. "So, how long did it take to get the upper hand?"

"Time, my dear. A lot of patience too." She smiled at Brina and set the tea down in front of her. "Now, tell me what happened."

Brina wasn't sure if she should. Amber Knight would probably side with her son. "He tried to stop me from doing my job."

"And what job are you doing?" Amber asked her quietly.

"I was called to Witch's Hollow. The dead want the murders to stop." Brina waited to see what Amber would say.

"It's about time." Amber's eyes met hers. "The men, they often fear for our safety. It's the feral part of their nature. Much harder to beat that out of them than one might think."

Brina choked on her tea and sputtered slightly. "Excuse me."

"Not that I want to see my son beat, but it might have to come to that." Amber smirked slightly. "I have an idea."

"What?"

"Stay here," she suggested.

"Here?" Brina was trying to figure out what the logic was behind that. Was she trying to keep them apart? Had she gone back a few steps?

"Men sometimes come around when we refuse them."

"You mean...? Oh my." She couldn't believe his mother was trying to talk to her about sex with her son. Brina blushed and looked away from her.

"Come now. Don't be shy. It's a natural thing. I also live in a house full of men. I've heard far more about their sex lives than anyone ever should. They seem to forget the walls are thin here." Amber sighed dramatically.

Brina giggled. Amber Knight was definitely growing on her. "Poor woman."

"Yes, do take pity on me. Maybe you'll have daughters." Amber looked wistful for a moment. "Then we can pass our heritage down to them. If you'd let me help...."

"Of course. But those are all hypothetical children at this point. I mean, it's not like...." Brina stopped talking and bit her lip. "Anyway, the problem at hand. He refused to let me follow the trail."

"Witch's Hollow?" she asked her.

"Yes. There was fresh blood on the altar, and the ley lines seemed to be lit up unusually."

"That's not a good sign. Every time that happens, we lose another witch."

"Even more reason to get to the bottom of it. We have to protect them." Brina slapped the table with her hand.

"I agree. But when a Knight first mates he has trouble thinking rationally. The only way to bring him around is to deny that which he craves."

"You're wicked," accused Brina with a smile.

"I've been there before, dear girl. You have to keep the upper hand with these men sometimes." Amber smiled and patted her hand.

"I think I could use a night away from him," agreed Brina.

"Good. Now tell me, how can I help with your case?"

"Did you keep records of the deaths?" Brina asked hopefully.

"You bet your ass I did." Amber smiled at her. "Come out to my office."

"Of course." Brina carried her cup of tea in her hand as she followed Amber out to the room where she had sat with her earlier.

"Sit, sit." Amber gestured to the small wicker chair next to the long coffee table.

Brina watched her pulled two plastic crates to the table. "That's a lot."

"They're all in here, too. All the notes I've taken. Interviews with some of the witches in the area. They don't like to talk to outsiders."

"I've spoken to Marina already."

"Really? She's a cantankerous one. She must have thought highly of you to talk to you at all." Amber smiled at her. "I've only met her twice."

"Must be my charm." Brina shrugged her shoulders. Or all the stars just aligned at the same time.

"Not just charm. You've got a pretty strong aura. Strong hereditary, I see." Amber was taking in her aura. "You do seem to have a few holes in your aura. We should do something about that."

"I ran into something nasty yesterday. Worst psychic attack in a long time. It was my fault really, though. I was distracted. When I went to Witch's Hollow, I kept my guard up this time. I did hear the voice though. I'm pretty sure he's working with something evil. A demon, perhaps?" Brina shivered just thinking about the long list of demons that were roaming the earth, creating pain and horror everywhere they touched. She'd helped banish a handful, and bound a few people who had been dabbling in the dark arts. It was safe to say her life was never boring.

"Let's get that aura cleaned up, then. We don't want him to get his fingers on you again."

"Agreed." Brina shivered slightly as she remembered how close he had come to ending her life. She'd barely had time to process it, as her world had seemed to spin out of control ever since. No thanks to Killian. She knew she loved him, but right now Brina wanted to lash out at him for trying to keep her from doing something she was destined to do. He had said she could still work. Clearly, he had no real idea what her work entailed.

Brina sifted through the files while Amber worked on cleansing her aura. Brina breathed in the sage as it floated over her. She was surrounded with different stones that were helping restore the right vibrations to her. Brina was starting to feel a little calmer, but she refused to let go of the anger that hummed inside her. Heaven help Killian if he tried to talk to her right now. The hair rose on the back of her neck just thinking about it.

"That should do it." Amber snuffed out the sage and said a quiet blessing over her.

"Thank you."

"Any time. Did you see anything?" Amber asked her.

"Yes. See here? The witches all have a profile." She pointed to the photos of the women in the folders. "None of them were born here. They were between the ages of twenty-six and twenty-nine. Most were dark haired."

"Like you?" The woman crossed her arms over her chest. "I don't like the sound of this, Brina."

"Don't worry. I'm not planning on doing anything stupid." Brina gave her a weak smile. His mother was right. She did fit the profile.

"I don't know how I didn't notice that before." Amber had a worried look on her brow.

"Sometimes it takes a fresh pair of eyes. Besides, this is what I do. Spirit sends me, and I dig into the details to find something that might help."

"How are we going to use this information?

"I'm not sure yet. It might come down to the first victim, Lydia Stern." Brina tapped her finger on the photo. "Would the women at camp remember her?"

"Perhaps."

"I'd like to go there tomorrow if I can." Brina wondered if that would even be possible.

"The boys were planning to go there soon. Maybe...."

Brina sighed. "That would mean I had to be on speaking terms with him, though."

"True. Something will work out. Goodness, it's almost dinner time. Care to help me?"

"Sure." It had been a long time since she'd cooked with anyone else in the kitchen. What could it hurt?

Chapter 19

Standing by Amber's side was actually pretty cathartic. She was reminded of the times she had spent in the kitchen with her own mother, who had passed away six years ago. Brina had been devastated by her loss, but the pain had lessened over the years.

"Tell me about your family, Brina." Amber was peeling a potato over the sink.

"I don't have any that I'm aware of. My mother left this world when I was twenty-two. Cancer."

"That's horrible. I'm so sorry, dear. You were just a child."

Brina smirked. Funny how that might have been an insult to her at the time, but right now Brina heartily agreed with her. She had just graduated college with a degree in sociology, one that she never got around to using in a technical field. Although, honestly, knowing how people functioned and coped had helped her in her investigations. This made them more human, and not just mere photos at the end of a file. Sometimes it helped her figure out the motive behind murder, too. Not that she ever really got credit for the work she did. She was known around the paranormal ring, just not in any actual legal capacity. Brina had called in a tip here or there to help an investigation, but she had usually remained anonymous. She didn't do it for prestige. Brina did it because somebody had to.

"I used to cook with my mom when I came home on the weekends. She wanted to make sure I was eating a home cooked meal at least once a week," Brina offered up.

"That's very important. I worry Kendrick isn't eating well when he's gone too."

"Kendrick? I haven't met him yet."

"He's in school right now. Getting his masters in anthropology." Amber beamed in pride.

"Fascinating. My degree is in sociology."

"Interesting."

"Not really," giggled Brina. "But it was the only thing that was palatable at the time."

"Not everyone is meant for college. Take the rest of the brood. Kam went into the reserves. He's finally off duty."

Well, that explained the bigger build. "That had to be hard."

"It was, but now that he's home, I feel the worst is over." Amber brought the potatoes over to chop. "Killian, he was always building things from the moment he could move the blocks around on the floor. He's been pretty successful."

"He's very talented." Brina smiled despite herself.

"Karter took ownership of the bar in town. His business

model has done so well, he sold it to a franchise. He still owns the first one, Glamz."

"Glamz?" Brina smiled. She was actually familiar with the place. "I've been to one. Love the paranormal touch."

"Haunted items seem to bring people in droves." Amber grinned. "If only they knew what other oddities were involved."

"What about Kyle?"

"He does landscaping. Keeps him busy and out of trouble."

"Does he get in a lot of trouble?" Brina asked curiously.

"Oh, heavens yes. They all do. Although, Killian has been the one I've had to worry about the least. That's probably why he was chosen as alpha of the pack. Now that Kenton is in...." She looked around to make sure her husband was not around. "His senior years, he is retiring his rank."

"That must have been a difficult decision." Brina had trouble seeing Killian retiring any time soon. He still had a lot wildness inside him, and the need to control everything and everyone around him. Killian was going to have to learn to get over disappointment.

"All right, let's get this in the oven. Why don't you go freshen up, Brina? I'm sure the boys will be here soon."

"Good idea." Brina headed up to the purple room where she had stayed the first night, and where she would stay tonight, because she did not plan on returning to the cabin with him later. Killian was going to have to learn that he was going to have to back down just a little.

Too bad she didn't have any of her clothes with her. She

wanted to make it as painful as possible for him. She undid the top two buttons of her shirt, hoping that just a little cleavage would make him squirm a little. Brina walked to the bathroom and found the lavender in the closet. She crushed some of it in her hands and wiped it around her neck. Then she puffed her hair up slightly to give it a little more volume. Siren. That's what she wanted to be. Strong enough to pull him in and push him away. Let him feel her fury for a change.

Brina heard voices downstairs, and she knew that Killian had returned. She felt his presence almost as if he were right there in the room with her. That didn't mean she was going to come down the stairs to greet him. Brina waited a good twenty minutes before she bothered to make her presence known, and when she did, she walked right past him and kissed his father on the cheek.

"Thank you for your help earlier."

Kenton flinched slightly, then a small grin worked its way across his face. "Of course, dear girl. Always ready to help a damsel in distress."

"Bri...." Killian called her name softly, but Brina ignored it.

"Excuse me, boys. I'm going to see if Mother needs any help." Mother. She threw that in just to keep him guessing, but saying it felt nice.

A round of laughter rose in the air behind her as the brothers teased Killian yet again. The fact that she was the cause only made her smile even more. When she saw Amber pulling out plates, she walked over to help her. "Do you mind if I call you Mother?"

Amber nearly dropped a plate. "My dear girl, of course not."

Brina gave her a warm hug. "I'd like to have a mother again."

Amber sniffed slightly. "Oh, don't make me cry, dear."

"Never show weakness?" Brina asked her.

"Never. Those boys will eat you alive. Best to stick to anger unless you really want to keep them guessing. Tears are the last line of defense with the Knights. They are defenseless to them, but you have to wear them down first."

Brina giggled. "Well, I don't plan on crying any time soon."

Amber looked her over. "Got your war paint on?"

"So to speak." Brina was determined to not break down.

"Good. An alpha needs an equal. Make sure you remember that," Amber cautioned her.

"He won't know what hit him." Brina crossed her heart with her fingers.

"Guarantee there's already a bet to see who's going to win this."

"How much you got on me?"

Amber laughed so loud, the plates rattled on the counter. "Oh, honey. I only bet on sure things."

"And?"

"It's four to one so far. They seem to think he'll wear you down."

"And you?" Brina waited to see what side she stood on.

"I know better." She winked at Brina and pulled her shirt down a little lower, then ran to get some oil from the windowsill. She dabbed a drop on Brina's skin and rubbed it in. "My grandmother's recipe."

Brina smelled lavender and honey. "That's beautiful."

"I'll make you a batch."

"I would love that. Shall I set the table?"

"Thank you, dear."

When Brina walked into the dining room, she saw Killian's eyes on her. As she lowered the plates onto the table, she bent over lower than usual, exposing the valley of her breasts to him. She didn't have to look at him to know whether or not he noticed. Brina had his full attention. When Karter entered the room, Killian quickly caught his attention.

"Karter, why don't you get the glasses?"

Brina smiled to herself. Killian didn't want his brothers to see. He was and always would be possessive of her. That didn't matter to her really, because no matter how he felt about it, she was her own person. She tried to walk into the other room, but Killian stood in her way.

"Bri, we need to talk."

Brina's eyes met his. "I have nothing to say to you, Killian."

His growl was so quiet no one else could have heard it. Nevertheless, Brina was not going to let it get to her.

"Stop being a bully, Killian."

Brina side stepped him and went out the other door that entered the living room instead of the kitchen. She could sense his anger, but knew he was not going to make a complete idiot of himself in front of his family. When she made her way into the kitchen, Brina saw the reassuring smile that Amber gave her.

"Stay the course."

"Aye, aye, Captain." She gestured to the food. "Can I carry something out?"

"Good idea. Not too high, though." Amber's face was filled with mischief as she gestured to Brina's cleavage.

Brina was glad she had at least one person on her side. She was sure that all the men thought it was their job to rule over the den, but they had a lot to learn about women. The only one who seemed smart enough to stay out of it was Kenton Knight, and that was probably because he already had a lifetime of experience with his mate. Killian was just getting started, and boy was he in for a surprise.

Brina set the food on the table and saw several pairs of eyes on her. Most were trained to her face, but at least two pairs had been distracted. Brina wasn't surprised to see Karter looking too, but he was harmless. His attention had the desired effect though, because she heard a loud "Stop!" and saw Karter visibly flinch, then look away.

Brina sat down in one of the empty seats, making sure not to sit next to Killian. Instead, she sat between Kyle and Kam in what she thought might have been Kendrick's seat. She turned to Kam and started talking to him.

"Kam, your mother was telling me about your time in the military. It must have been hard being away from home."

Kam was taking a drink of his water, which he gulped down almost painfully as Killian's eyes were on him. "It had its moments."

"I'm glad you made it home." She smiled at him.

"Uh…thanks." He held one hand in front of him as if to deflect Killian's glare.

"Kyle, did you design the garden out back?"

Kyle smirked at Killian and turned to smile at her. "Yes, I did. How did you know?"

"Well, I'm pretty observant. When your mother told me you did landscaping, it reminded me of the garden outside. I can feel your touch there."

Karter nearly choked on his food. Killian started to pound him much harder on the back than he needed to. Karter held a hand up. "I'm good. It just went down the wrong pipe."

"Sure you're okay? I'm certified in CPR and first aid."

"NO! No…I'm good." He answered quickly, and looked over at Killian with raised eyebrows.

Brina sighed. She ate her food slowly, enjoying every single bite. When she had eaten half her food, she realized that Killian had barely touched his. Instead, he was angrily moving it around his plate. "Karter, I hear you're behind the wildly successful Glamz. I've been to the one in Boston, although that was a few years ago. Great place for single ladies to—"

Karter interrupted her before she continued. This time he seemed to be throwing his hat into the ring, as if to say "What the hell…why not?" "I'd be happy to show you the club in town. It's not as hopping as Boston, but we do a fair amount of business."

"I'd like that." She gave him a sweet smile.

Killian put his napkin on his plate and pushed away from the table. Brina watched him leave the room without an inch of remorse. She smirked and looked over at Amber, who was nodding at her in approval.

"Well, that was intense. Are you trying to get me killed?" Karter asked her.

Brina giggled. "He wasn't going to hurt you. Besides, if he did, he'd have me to deal with."

"Oh?" Karter's eyebrow raised in curiosity.

"Nobody messes with my family." Her chin held high, she made her feelings known. "Now, if you don't mind, I think I've made my point."

"Not staying here?" Amber asked her.

"Oh no, thank you, but the battle's just beginning. Time to bring it home." Brina smiled at her.

"Man, I'd hate to be him right now," Kyle whistled.

"Liar," Karter interjected. "We'd all like to be him. No offense, Brina, but you're one hell of a catch."

"None taken, and just so there's no confusion. There was never a chance with any of you. No offense." Brina reached over and patted Karter on the hand specifically. The rest of the room broke into an uproar of laughter.

Brina stood up and sighed softly as she left the room. She had heard the outside door close, so she knew he was no longer in the house. Time to drive her point home once and for all.

Chapter 20

The night had just started to make its presence known to the world around it when Brina left the house. She knew Killian was furious, but he had a lesson to learn whether he wanted to admit or not. Turnabout was fair play, after all. When she found him sitting on the bench in the garden, she smiled to herself. He looked so rigid, so withdrawn.

"Killian?"

"So, now you're talking to me?" His voice was definitely angry. Served him right.

"If I choose to. I *am* my own person." She moved in front of him and stood with her arms crossed. Her eyes met his.

"You're mine." His eyes flashed angrily.

"I'm not a possession, Killian. I am a living, breathing person, and if you think you are going to spend a lifetime ordering me around, you have another think coming." She was ready to spit nails.

"God, you're sexy when you're mad." Desire was

definitely on his mind.

"Too bad for you then, I guess." Brina wanted to rip her hair out, she was so angry with him.

"It doesn't have to be."

"Do you know I had a life before you?" Brina ignored the heat coming off from him. Even in her anger she wanted every inch of him.

"Yes, but—"

"My job is important, Killian. If you take that away from me, I have nothing." Her face was flushed.

"You still have me." His voice was soft, almost haunting.

"What did you give up?" She challenged him.

"I...." He looked thoughtful. "My sanity."

Brina turned around and stomped back into the house, letting the door slam behind her. She didn't even look for the others. Instead, she raced up to the purple room and locked the door behind her. She grabbed one of the pillows from the bed and crammed it into her face so she could scream at the top of her lungs.

She heard his footsteps on the stairs, followed by a loud pounding on the door, but she refused to open it. Instead, she put the pillow over her head and tried to block out the noise.

"Brina, if you don't let me in right now, I'm going to knock this door down," he threatened.

"Killian Ian Knight!" A loud female voice interrupted him. "I've taught you better than that."

Brina smirked. Watch him squirm for a minute. He deserved it. Killian hadn't even wanted to talk about compromise. Brina might have been able to handle that, but it had never been breached.

"Mother, we need to talk." Killian's voice was still angry, but held a quieter tone to it.

"Talk? You're practically ripping the door off the hinges. That is *not* how you treat a lady. You also do not order her around. You are not her boss. You are her *equal*. I thought I raised you better than that. You need to get yourself under control." Amber's voice was still coming in hot.

"She won't see reason." Killian sounded like he was now leaning against the door.

"Reason? So, what is your reason?" Amber was now tapping her foot loudly on the floor.

"I'm trying to keep her safe."

Brina shivered at the words. She did understand what he was saying. There was a fair amount of danger out there in the woods, but she had been sent here to erase it.

"That very well may be, but you cannot break someone's spirit, Killian. It's who she is." Amber's voice was filled with emotion. "Give her time."

"I love her." His voice sounded ragged and hurt.

That was enough to break through her anger. Brina walked over to the door and unlocked it. When she opened it, he nearly fell inside. Brina held up a hand to keep him steady. "Are you ready to listen?"

He turned to look at her with a softer expression on his face. "Yes."

"Good. Let's take a walk."

Brina stepped around him and nodded to his mother. Brina knew she didn't want to see her son in anguish either, but at least she had been on her side. One thing she had learned for sure, Killian was a tempest. He needed to be tempered and softened on his hard edges if they were going to have any kind of future together. She may have promised to be his and no one else's, but that didn't mean she had to stick around and put up with him when he was trying to master her. There were times she would let him, but on this, she could not let up.

She didn't even wait for him to catch up to her. Brina found the marker and started to follow it back to the cabin. When she heard his breath behind her, Brina sighed slowly and turned around to look at him. Her heart skipped a beat when she saw the moon shine down on his face. Every inch of her wanted to reach out and touch him, but she refused to give in to it.

"Killian...."

"I've been overbearing."

His words surprised her. "And?"

"I will try not to do so in the future, but I'm worried about you."

"I know." She looked away. "People are going to die."

"You could die." His voice was almost inaudible. "I just found you, Brina."

Brina felt a tear slide from the corner of her eye. She reached over and touched his face. "I know you're scared."

The truth of the matter was she would feel the exact same way if it were him going up against this unknown entity. His lips turned to kiss her hand.

"I know I'm a brute. Maybe it's the alpha in me." He gave

her a half-smile.

"An alpha needs an alpha," Brina pointed out. "I have to push back sometimes, Killian. But, there are compromises that could be made."

"Oh?"

"If you're so afraid for me, then help me. I want to find him, but I'm not stupid. I have no plans to attack him, or to even try to face him on my own." Brina pulled her hand away and put it on his arm.

"I thought you were trying to—"

"Clearly you made an assumption. This is why we need to communicate, not shut down."

"You're a lot like my mother," Killian accused her.

"Good. I rather like her." She smiled at him. "If your work allows, I'd like to visit the witch's camp. I'd be happy for the company."

"I'll take you tomorrow afternoon after I finish up some of my work," Killian agreed.

"There. See. Was that really so hard?" She started to continue her walk through the woods.

"Where are you going?" Killian asked her.

"I guess you'll find out when we get there." Brina smirked at him.

"Bri...." His voice was gruff when he realized they were now standing outside the cabin.

"Yes, Kilian. We're home. For as long as it suits us. And if you want to know what happens after a fight, you'll come inside."

She bit her bottom lip and walked inside. Brina wasn't

surprised to see he followed her in right away. Brina turned around to see him stalking her, but she held up her hand.

"Ah-ah. You don't get to do that. Tonight, I make the calls."

He shivered visibly. "Am I being punished?"

"Hmm...if you want to go that route, I guess I'll just go to sleep." She turned and started to head to the stairs, but his hands pulled her back.

"So, what was option two?" He looked almost desperate for her, and she hadn't even started yet.

Tonight, Brina was going to take her lesson just a little bit further. It was risky, considering she had never done anything like what she had planned, but somehow, she knew it would be a night he wouldn't soon forget. "You don't get to be alpha here."

He gulped, and the golden light that flashed through his eyes seemed to be even brighter. "What if I'm not prepared for that?"

Brina started to remove her clothing, one piece at a time. When she was completely naked before him, he stepped toward her and she held up a hand. "No touching."

"Bri...," he grumbled.

"I'm in control here, Killian. Put your beast on a leash," she cautioned him as she reached down to slide his belt from his jeans. His hands flinched at his sides, but he didn't move.

Her hand slid beneath his shirt and she scratched her nails along his abdomen. Desire ripped through her when she felt him clench beneath her.

"Take your shirt off, Killian," she ordered him. When he

started to go too fast, she interrupted him. "Slowly...."

Brina watched the shirt reveal every inch of him as he slid it up his body. She licked her lips, and thought about which part she would explore first. Brina stepped closer and knelt down before him. She licked his skin around his navel, and slowly worked her way up his body, letting her skin touch his at random intervals. Anytime her nipples touched his flesh, Killian sucked in his breath. She saw his hands clenched into fists at his sides. He was fighting for self-control.

Brina reached up and bit his ear before whispering into it. "Lose the pants and come upstairs."

Brina left him where he stood as she walked upstairs to their room. She looked over at the bed and smiled. Four posters, excellent. She went into the closet and looked for anything she could use for the next stage of his torture. Brina found a few silken cords that must have been used to tie back the older curtains. She smiled brightly. "Perfect."

When she came back into the room, Killian was standing in front of the doorway in all his naked glory. Her heart skipped a beat and she almost lost all resolve. Closing her eyes, she reminded herself that this wasn't as much about sex as it was about teaching him that she could be his equal—she could take control.

"Get on the bed, Killian."

He moved slowly, like a creature that stalked in the night. When he sat on the bed, he looked up at her with a rueful grin. "So...?"

"Lay down. Arms up." Brina unraveled one of the cords in her hand.

"What are you doing, Bri?" He looked slightly nervous.

"Are you afraid of me?" Brina asked her.

"*Never.*" He lay back against the pillows and held his hands up.

She quickly tied one of his arms to the post of the bed. When she leaned too close to him, he took her nipple into his mouth. Brina moaned and felt desire shoot through her body. She pulled away from him and ran her nails across his stomach. Small angry welts were already starting to form. "Did I say you could touch me?"

Sparks exploded behind his eyes, and his voice was a low rumble. "No."

Brina repeated the process with his other hand and looked down at him. "Hmm....choices, choices. Should I do the legs too?"

Killian gulped and his stomach seemed to tremble at the thought. Seeing his excitement, Brina decided to go for broke. She retrieved more cord and tied both legs to the bottom posts. When she was done, she looked down at him with a satisfied smile. "I think I have you just where I want you."

"Oh?" Killian was thoroughly excited. His cock stood up at attention. Brina was sure his mind was filled with all the things she might do to him.

Brina smiled and left the room. She heard him calling for her and chuckled. Let him think she had left him. What she really was doing was looking for something to use on him. As she searched through the bathroom closets, she found exactly what she was looking for. Massage oil, with just a hint of heat. Part of her wondered what he was doing with it in his closet, but she'd get to that later.

Killian looked relieved when she came back into the room. Brina could see he had already struggled against the ties slightly. He would be chafed by the time she was done with him. She was sure he would forgive her. He might even thank her.

Brina opened the bottle and poured some in her hands. She straddled his hips and sighed when she felt his body squirm beneath her slightly. She let him get away with the cock that seemed to push into one of her ass cheeks. Leaning over so that her breasts were just over his face, she started to massage one arm. Every so often her nipple would land right against his mouth, but she would pull away before he could kiss it. She repeated the process with the other arm.

When she brought her mouth down to his, his kiss was ragged and wild. Brina pulled away so her lips were just out of his reach. He struggled against his ropes slightly. Brina tapped him on the nose. "Ah-ah."

She licked his lips and he sucked in his breath. Her fingers slid down and tweaked one of his nipples. It was as hard as concrete below her.

"Kiss me, Killian."

Brina did not have to ask him twice. His mouth devoured hers with a wildness that was matched only by her own need. And while she knew it would be easy to give in to it, there was still much more to do.

Breaking away from the kiss, she poured more oil into her hands. "Good boy."

He smirked at her. "I'm not a...oh."

Brina had moved down to his legs. With her mouth near his cock, she licked the tip before drawing it slowly into her mouth. She massaged his legs and felt him quiver beneath her. His entire body seemed to stiffen beneath her. Brina released him and licked her lips. "You taste good, Killian."

His hands tried to rip the ropes off the bed posts, but all he did was hurt himself. "Bri."

She finished up her massage and looked up at him. "Am I not taking good care of you, Killian?"

"Oooo...." He shivered when she licked her lips.

"What's the matter, Killian? If you don't like this, we can stop." Brina was about to climb off him when he shivered.

"I might die if you stop. He'll kill me." The yellow light was back, and it was burning deep inside him.

"Oh, well, we can't have that." Brina was so excited, and was already dripping. She straddled his hips, spreading her legs wide. When she lowered herself onto him, she felt his cock searing her core. So hot, hard, and definitely ready.

He tried to move his hips, but Brina squeezed his nipples hard. "Don't you dare move, Killian."

His entire body lay ramrod still, as much as it pained him to do so. Brina moved up and down slowly, running her hands up and down his chest as she did so. She took what she wanted, but she couldn't quite get herself there. The heat inside her continued to build relentlessly.

"Please...," she whispered.

His hips started to move slowly on the bed under her. She felt her desire rise dangerously inside her. "Don't you dare finish, Killian Knight."

He growled softly, but she saw the tightness in his body as he tried to rein himself in. Brina rode the length of him faster and harder. Throwing her head back, she let her hair cascade around her shoulders as ecstasy took over. When her orgasm hit, Brina felt like every inch of her exploded. She felt him stiffen as he tried to follow her rules. Sensing his need, Brina denied it. She climbed off him and tried to keep her wits about her.

"Witch," he complained.

"Beast," she countered. Brina leaned over and took him in her mouth again. She could taste her desire on him. Brina bit him hard and released him. Climbing up the length of him, she whispered in his ears, "You taste like me now." Killian growled and thrashed under her. Brina whispered in his ear again. "Would you like a taste?"

"God, yes." His voice was frenzied until she brought her mouth down to his. His mouth took every inch of hers as his tongue sought to retrieve the scent of her desire.

Pulling away from him, she whispered in his other ear. "Are you going to be a good boy, Killian?"

"Yes...."

"Had enough torture?" Her eyes met his. She could tell he was conflicted. He wanted to let himself be wild and free with her, but he also enjoyed her taming him. He shivered and she took pity on him. She slowly untied his legs. Then she undid the bindings of his hands.

The moment he was free, he pulled her down to him. His mouth translated the need coursing through him. When he broke the kiss, he looked up at her. "I'm wild for you."

"So is he." She ran a nail across his chest and saw that his eyes only confirmed it. "I concede to you for now, Killian. Take what you want."

Killian's nails raked across her back in reply. He moved her over his cock and pushed into her molten lava core. His hands reached up to squeeze her breasts as she rode his length like a cowgirl riding a bronco. Her back arched as her orgasm took her breath away.

When she thought he would give in and finish, he tossed her off of him and moved her onto her fours. Brina felt a ripple of desire fill her core. His beast and he wrestled for control before he slid into her. His fingers squeezed her ass painfully as he started to drive himself into her, man and beast, their souls wanting one thing — to find their pleasure in her heat. Arching her back, she felt him slide further in. As he drove into her, she ached for each thrust. When he slammed into her one last time, they erupted together.

She pouted when he slid out of her. Collapsing on the bed, she tried to catch her breath. Killian rolled her around and kissed her hard on the lips. Sighing against him, she wrapped her arms around his neck. When he broke the kiss, she smiled.

"I love you, Killian Knight."

"I don't deserve you." He looked shaken with her words.

"Probably not, but now you're stuck with me."

He pulled her into his arms and they lay there in the silence. Brina broke it with her next question.

"So, what did you learn today?"

"Never underestimate you."

"Anything else?"

"Happy mate, happy fate."

Brina sighed. "And don't you forget it, Killian."

"I shall endeavor to only piss you off enough to make you take advantage of me." He slapped her ass with his hand.

"Learn to yield, Killian. You might find some of it rewarding." She reached up and squeeze his nipple with her hand before twisting it.

"Ouch! Uncle! Uncle! Okay...I get it." He held his hands up in defense.

"Good boy."

He chuckled loudly beneath her. "Do I get a treat now?"

"Not unless you can manifest the energy for it." She nodded down to the deflated erection.

"I'm going to have to give him a stern talking to."

"Want me to try?" She licked her lips and pushed up to her elbows.

"Woman...get some sleep. You're going to need it," he warned her.

Brina snuggled close to him and sighed in contentment. She was starting to feel tired. Maybe just a little nap.

Chapter 21

As Brina slept, images rotated inside her brain. She saw the gleam of a knife before it sliced down through the air. A scream echoed around inside her mind, and she saw Marina's face flash in her head. She was in trouble. Her eyes opened and she sucked in her breath.

Where was Killian? Morning light was just starting to filter through the window. She reached over to touch the bed, and it was cold to the touch. Her heart beat erratically in her chest. Something was wrong. She raced to the closet and threw on some clothes. Running down the stairs, she looked all over the cabin for him. She saw a note on the counter.

Had to take care of something. Stay here.

Stay here? Was he kidding her? Had they not already talked about this? Marina was in danger, and the longer she waited for him to get back, the harder it would be to help her. Should she go find the others?

Brina felt her insides twist. It might already be too late.

She picked up her phone and looked to see if she could get a signal. Maybe she could call the house. No signal. Damn it.

Brina scribble on the note. *Someone's in trouble. I had to help. Find me.*

She knew he would find her, and when he did Killian would probably threaten to lock her up and throw away the key. She'd deal with the consequences later. Brina retrieved anything that might be useful. Holy water, sea salt, pepper spray, her small pocketknife that she kept on her, she put all of these things in her jacket pockets, hoping that she wouldn't have to use any of them.

When she walked outside, she could sense the heaviness in the air. She saw a white light near the edge of the forest and knew it was a sign. Brina followed the orb as it shot through the air. The further it went into the woods, the more she was starting to second guess her choices.

While she thought it would lead her to Witch's Hollow, she was surprised to find it was not taking her there at all. By the time she realized her mistake, Brina was lost within the forest. She should have marked her path to help her find her way out. There was nothing to do about that now.

The orb of light was slowing down, its glow fading to a small pinpoint of light. The trees around her seemed to be devoid of life. A cold chill ran up her spine, and she felt the same energy as she had from the man that had called to her across the glen. As she continued on, she saw a small, old shack. The roof was rusted and the windows were covered in grime.

Walking around it, she almost gasped when she saw

crimson spots on the ground before the door. Fresh blood. Brina shivered. This was the place. She walked over to the window and peered inside. She never heard the footsteps behind her until it was too late.

"Witch!" the voice accused, right before something hard slammed against her head. The lights turned off around her, and Brina slipped into a darkness that she could not claw her way out of.

When Brina did finally come to, her head was throbbing painfully. Her vision was blurry as she tried to get it to come into focus. Was she still inside the shack? As her eyes started to adjust, she saw shelves filled with objects that made no sense to her. Effigies? Body parts? Was that a human tongue? Brina shivered and a tear made its way down her face.

Get it together, Brina. This was not the time to freak out. Albeit, this was definitely the worst-case scenario she had put herself into. If she ever got out of this, Killian would never let her hear the end of it. That was one thing she was sure of.

As she looked around the other side of the room, she saw a lifeless figure on the floor. Was that Marina? Brina tried to get up, but her hands were tied to her feet. A slow murmur sounded from the body, and Brina gave a sigh of relief.

"Marina?"

Only a moan answered her. Brina inched closer, her feet sliding across the floor as she tried to get the rest of her to follow. She only ended up falling over on her side. Her face slammed into the floor, and she saw spots behind her head.

"Damn it."

"*Brina?*" The woman's whisper seemed painful and

broken.

"Yes. I'm here. Marina?"

"Yes. He's going to come back," Marina warned her.

"Who?"

"James Morgen."

Brina wondered who that was. She'd never seen the name in all the files. "Is he a caster?"

"I don't think so. He enjoys inflicting physical pain." Marina flinched as if she were remembering the torture.

"Who's drowning the witches?"

"The demon he's working with. They both hate us. The more he kills, the more power the demon gains."

"We have to banish him. But first, we need to get out of here." Brina knew they had to leave, but neither one of them would be able to get out of here unless Brina could get herself untied. There was only one thing to do, and while it would hurt, there was no way around it.

Brina closed her eyes and let the energy inside her flow into her hands. She sent everything she had and conjured a ball of flame. The small fire started to burn the ropes around her. As the fire crackled into it, she felt her flesh start to sizzle in protest. When the ties were free, she put out the small fire that erupted on the old wooden floor. Slightly singed, she rubbed her skin briefly before leaning over to check on Marina.

"We've got to get out of here, Marina. He'll be back soon."

"You have to go without me."

"Not happening."

Brina leaned over and her head pounded. She put a hand to her head and felt a large gash that was still bleeding.

Ignoring it, she knew the only way either one of them was going to get out of this alive was if they found their way out of here.

Brina untied Marina as quickly as she could, but the knots were hard to work free. She struggled with them until she finally was able to get them. "Can you walk?"

"I can try," Marina didn't seem all that confident. Her body was in pretty bad shape. Her face was covered in cuts and bruises. Her clothing was covered in blood.

"Up we go, Marina." Brina pulled her up, ignoring the added pressure it put on her head. When Marina was standing, Brina slid her arm around her. Kicking the door open, Brina helped her along the best that she could. They had barely made it a few feet before an angry voice erupted.

"And just where do you think you're going?" Brina turned when she heard the click of a gun.

"You don't have to do this."

"All you witches need to die. You're responsible." He spat on the ground as if the thought of them disgusted him.

"I don't know what you think we're responsible for, but—"

"Murdering heathens!" he accused them. He shook his gun in the air in emphasis. "Conjuring devastation to the world around us. If you hadn't brought the flood, they'd still be alive."

Brina had no idea what he was talking about. No witch she knew would ever want to destroy the earth with a flood, especially if doing so would kill any living thing. "You're mistaken."

"Am I, witch?" His eyes went wilder, and Brina saw the dark phantom she had seen a few days before. It seemed to whisper in his ear, driving him further into the depths of his craziness.

A small spark erupted from Marina's hands as she pushed away from Brina. "I banish thee, thy evil from this world."

It was like time stood still. She saw the blasting spark from Marina's hands as she shot at the phantom, and a burst of light emptying from the man's gun. Brina jumped in front of Marina at the last second. Her body jolted when the bullet hit her.

A series of loud growls erupted around them as a flash of fur lunged past her. The man barely had a chance as four enraged wolves tore into his flesh. His screams of terror lasted only seconds.

Brina turned to see the phantom floating above her, the demon in disguise. She used the rest of her energy to send a glaring light at the evil creature above her, the demon that had caused so much death to the world around them. "I banish thee, they evil from this world."

The blast of energy was all she had left before she collapsed on the ground. Her entire back burned and ached. She put her hand against it and felt hot liquid flowing against it.

"Killian?" she whispered as her head dropped to the ground.

~*~

"Damn it, Brina!" Killian scooped her up in his arms. "I told you to stay home.

"Killian?" Kam called over to him. "What should we do?"

Killian turned to look at his brother in anguish. He had never felt so helpless in his life. At this moment his alpha had turned off, as every inch of him mourned for the woman in his arms. She was still alive, but for how long?

"Killian...." Kam broke through again. "We can't leave him like this."

Killian looked over at the body they had just ripped to shreds. Kam was right. The only way to keep the pack safe was to keep their identity unknown. "Throw him in the shed and light it up."

Marina fell to her knees. "Bring her here, Knight."

Killian was loath to move her, but if the witch could help her, he would take his chances. Brina whimpered in his arms as he moved her. It broke his heart into fractured pieces to see her in such pain.

"Please...."

"I'll do what I can, Knight. We need to stop the bleeding." Marina ripped some of her shirt and held it tightly against the wound. "Hold this."

More ripping sounded as Marina made small strips. She wound it around Brina's shoulder, making it as tight as possible. "There will be questions if you take her to the hospital."

"What do you suggest?" Killian held her tightly to his body, and kissed her head as she moaned in her state of unconscious.

"Bring her to the camp. We can help her." Marina's eyes met his. "I know you love her. She saved my life, and sent that thing back to the hell it came from. We'll take good care

189

of her."

"Kyle."

"Yes, Killian." Kyle had just helped the others carry the body into the shack.

"Help...." For the life of him, Killian couldn't remember her name. He had met her before, but right now his brain was having trouble focusing on anything but the woman who seemed almost lifeless in his arms.

"Marina," she offered up her name.

"Help Marina walk. We're headed to the camp." Killian hoisted Brina up in his arms, holding her as close to his warmth as he could. She felt cold against him. They had to hurry.

"On it." Kyle helped her up and supported her weight. When she stumbled slightly, he caught her. "Easy, Marina. There you go."

The trek to the camp seemed to take an eternity. His wolf inside howled in despair, as if already mourning her loss, but Killian refused to believe it was over yet. If he had just stayed there, helped her with her quest to find the man who was torturing Witch's Hollow, maybe this would not have happened. Instead of including her in their hunt, he had left her out. They had the same goal, both of them, but Killian had not let her in. If she died, he would never forgive himself.

When they made it to the camp, Marina pointed to a long table. "Set her there."

Killian did not want to let her go, but he knew he had to. He lay her down as gently as possible, and shivered when she whispered his name. He ran his fingers through his hair and closed his eyes.

"Please don't let her die."

"I'll do my best."

Marina called for the others to come help her, and a flurry of activity bustled around the camp. A circle of women now surrounded Brina, blocking her from Killian's view.

His fear took over and he ran to the edge of the forest. He shifted into his wolf and ran as fast and far as his paws could carry him. He stood on his haunches and lifted his head into the air. A loud mournful wail erupted from him as the two of them mourned for their mate. She was still with him, but her chances...she had lost so much blood. Their lives would never be the same.

Killian?

She called to him from across the void he was sinking into, like a whisper on the wind. Did that mean...? Please don't let her be dead. He zipped through the forest, retracing his steps. When he made it to the camp, Brina was no longer on the table. He quickly shifted to his human form and called out for her. "Brina?"

"Relax, Killian." Kyle held out his hand to calm him down. "They've just moved her inside."

"Is she...?"

"Fine. She seems to be fine. They got the bullet out. No internal damage. They think the wound will heal."

"How long was I gone?" Killian shook his head in disbelief.

"Four hours." Kyle smirked at him.

Marina stepped out of one of the shelters. "Killian, she's

awake."

The color left his face. "She's awake?"

"Yes, and she's asking for you." Marina smiled softly. "Go easy on her. She's done a lot for us, Killian."

He felt his anger start to rise. "She shouldn't have—"

"Done what you would have done?" suggested Kyle.

Killian turned on his brother. "That's different. I'm—"

"An ass?" suggested Kyle.

"Kyle!" His hair started to rise at the base of his neck.

"You can't ask her to give up something that you wouldn't give up. It's only fair," Kyle pointed out.

"I...." Killian paused as Kyle's words sank in. He was right. The lesson of his life was right there in front of him. If he wanted to keep Brina safe, if her happiness mattered to him, he couldn't change her. "You're right. But don't let it go to your head. One day, you'll find a woman who will drive you insane."

"I should be so lucky." He patted his brother on the back. "Now you can go to her."

Killian followed Marina into the shelter and saw Brina on one of the beds. She looked so small against the pillows, and her face was incredibly pale. "Brina?"

Her eyes fluttered open. "Killian."

He knelt down beside her and kissed her softly on the cheek. "I thought I'd lost you."

Her lips wobbled slightly. "I'm sorry, Killian."

"You've nothing to be sorry for, love." He stroked the tears away from her face. "You can't stop who you are any more than I can stop myself."

"Is he...?"

"Gone. Yes. He won't be bothering anyone in this life again." He brought her hand to his face and kissed it softly.

"So is the demon, Brina. You've managed to destroy his claim over Witch's Hollow," Marina interjected from the side.

"Marina...are you all right?" Brina turned to look at her.

"I'll be right as rain soon, dear. As will you. I think you should rest here a few days and let the healers help you," Marina suggested.

Brina turned to look up at Killian. "Can we go home, Killian?"

"Love, it's better not to move you. I won't leave you," he promised her. They would have to pry his dead body away from her first. Killian was not going to let her out of his sight any time soon. "Rest, Brina."

Brina's eyes fluttered closed and she sighed softly. Killian turned to Marina with his eyes filled with tears. "Thank you."

"There's nothing we wouldn't do for your pack, Knight. And now, your mate. You've chosen well."

"Yes, yes I have."

Killian would never regret his decision. She might make his hair grey before its time, but that didn't matter. Life without her was impossible. He had never realized how little living he was doing until she walked into his life. She had wrecked any of his plans of bachelorhood right from the start. His brothers would be infinitely grateful to her, for that he was sure, but he was the lucky one.

193

Chapter 22

Brina sighed to herself as she glanced down into the gardens below. She was a very lucky woman. If Killian and his brothers had not come when they had, her life would have turned out differently. Walking to the mirror, she looked at the pink scar that was a reminder of how close she had come to losing her life. The women at the camp had done miraculous work. She would forever be thankful for their healing hands.

Brina looked herself over one more time. Her white dress flowed around her like a soft cloud of lace. Her hair was pulled up on top of her head and woven with small white flowers and sprigs of fresh lavender. With spring now in full force, it would be a beautiful day, with memories she would treasure deep inside her for the rest of her life.

Today, her world would change forever. Killian's too — he just didn't know it yet. She picked up her bouquet and the small box she had wrapped earlier — a gift that she had just discovered, one that would probably bring a tear to his eyes.

"Are you ready, Brina?" Kenton asked her from the hallway.

"Yes, *Dad*." She walked into the hall and kissed him on the cheek.

"You look beautiful." He smiled at her. "Killian's almost out of his mind."

"I'm not too late, am I?" She bit her lip.

"Not at all. You're right on time. He was just early. He's been barking out orders since he woke up this morning. He wanted everything to be perfect."

"But it is. I have everything I've ever dreamed of. Including a family to love." Brina smiled secretly.

"I think you're up to something," accused Kenton with a gleam in his eye.

"Always," she giggled.

"Go easy on him, Brina," cautioned Kenton.

"I'll be good." She held up a hand in promise.

"There you two are." Amber rushed over to her and took her other arm. "Can I hold this for you?"

Brina was holding the small bouquet and the box in one hand. "Yes. But I'll need it back after the ceremony. It's a gift for Killian."

"Let's go, dear." The door leading out to the garden was already open.

Brina looked down at the ground and saw hundreds of red petals scattered over the white roll of fabric that marked her path down the aisle. A gentle music played in the background, and the people before them rose to greet the sight of her on the steps. While Brina did not have a family of her own, over the past few months the witches of the camp had become her makeshift family. They had included her in their fold, and surrounded her with kinship and love. They were here to support the next step in her life.

Brina's eyes looked up to the front, where Killian was watching her with the most adoration she had ever seen in her life. His face was filled with so many emotions at once. She smiled at him and saw the light flash in his eyes. He was hers for eternity, or even longer if the fates had their way.

When she finally made it to his side, Killian reached for her hand and brought it to his lips. She smiled at him as her flesh trembled against his lips. Their eyes met and Brina's breath caught in her throat.

"Killian," she whispered.

The ceremony seemed to last forever, and while Brina enjoyed every single detail that Killian had painstakingly planned, she was anxious for it to be over. When he finally leaned down to kiss the bride, Brina was having trouble containing herself.

"You're up to something," he whispered in her ear.

"Yes." She smiled secretively. Brina reached for the box and held it up for him. "I have something for you."

"Brina, this isn't necessary —"

"Just open the damn box, Killian," she ordered him. Brina had learned that sometimes she had to use her bossy voice in order to get him to follow her directions.

"Fine, but I didn't get you anything, Brina." He gave her a guilty smile.

"But you did. Just open the box." Brina was bursting at

the seams. Now, everyone else around them was starting to talk in slow whispers as they tried to figure out what was going on.

Killian untied the ribbon and slowly slid off the cover. When he looked inside his eyebrows rose. "Is this what I think it is?"

"Yep." She waited to see his reaction. Would he be happy? Or would he want to lock her up in a tower and protect her?

He held the small slip of paper in his hand and almost howled his joy. "We're having a baby!" Killian scooped her up in his arms and swung her into the air. Brina kissed him hard on the lips and held on tight.

A loud uproar sounded around them as everyone congratulated them. When Killian set her down, Brina turned to find his brothers were pulling out their wallets. They each handed money over to Amber Knight, who winked at Brina.

"You know I only bet on a sure thing."

Brina grinned at her and turned to look at her husband. "So, are you going to lock me up?"

"Nope."

"Really?" Brina was surprised.

"We're a team, Bri. I support you; you support me." Killian looked as if those words were killing him.

Brina decided to let him off the hook. "Killian, my love. My days of heading into the fray are over. I'll be more of a couch detective from here on out."

Relief washed across his face. "I love you, Bri."

"I love you too, Killian." She put a hand to her stomach and rubbed it gently. "Besides, this one's going to be a handful."

"How do you know that?" asked Killian.

"Have you met her father?" Brina grinned.

The men reached into their wallets again, and this time Kenton opened his hands. Brina shook her head. "Kenton Knight!"

"Hey, it had to happen eventually." He winked at her, and they all started to laugh again.

Brina snuggled against Killian and sighed. "Thank you."

"For what?" Killian kissed the top of her head.

"For choosing me."

Brina looked around her at all the blessings he had brought to her life. She would be forever thankful that her car had stopped working that night, although she was fairly certain Kenton Knight had something to do with that, seeing as how he had fixed it up right as rain with very little effort. She sighed in contentment as she snuggled against Killian.

About the Author

Ever since childhood, Elissa Daye has enjoyed reading stories as an escape from life. When she was a teenager she started to write her own stories that kept her entertained when she ran out of books to read. When she was accepted into Illinois Summer School for the Arts in her Junior year of High School, she knew she wanted to become a writer. Elissa graduated from Illinois State University in December 1999 with a Bachelor of Science in Elementary Education and began her teaching career, hoping to find moments to write in her free time.

After seven years of teaching, Elissa decided to focus on her writing and made the decision to put her teaching years behind her so that she could create the stories she had always dreamed of. She is now happily married and a stay at home mom, who writes in every spare moment she can find, doing her best to master the art of multitasking to get everything accomplished.

www.ingramcontent.com/pod-product-compliance
Lightning Source LLC
Chambersburg PA
CBHW030330180626
46810CB00003B/1303